The Jaguar's Quest

Sequel to
The Lost City

George Dismukes

I dedicate this and all my books to my soul mate, Nadine.

THE JAGUAR'S QUEST

ISBN: 978-1-953735-63-8

Melange Books, LLC
White Bear Lake, MN 55110
www.melange-books.com

Published in the United States of America.

Cover Design by Ashley Redbird Designs

CHAPTER ONE

Transition

"THE BRUTAL, UNVARNISHED TRUTH IS, WE, AS A HUMAN race have become suicidal. Yes, I said suicidal. In the recent past we managed to overcome a global pandemic because doctors and scientists were able to conduct research and find a vaccine. When the forests and jungles of this world are depleted and there isn't enough oxygen to breathe, there will be no cure, no vaccine you can inject in your arm to save you. Scientists and all the doctors in the world will not be able to help. You will desperately suck for a lung full of air, but it will not be there. You will die. This planet will shut down until the destroyed, depleted, denuded jungles of the world can regrow.

"If you do not like what I am saying. If it offends you. If it frightens you. Good! Then I've done what I came here to do. Now it's your turn. Take action! And the time to take action is *NOW*, not tomorrow, *NOW*!"

Brandon Shaw stood before a gathering of close to a thousand visitors. With him at the dais was Naja, his pet three-hundred-pound black jaguar, which in reality was closer to an alter-ego. And sitting only a few feet away at the presenter's table, was Andrea, the woman who had cleaved to Brandon in contradiction to everything that was supposed to be real about her life. She had fallen madly in love with this jungle man and in so doing, saved him from some serious foolishness he had gotten himself involved in.

But in so doing, she had also gone against her original mission. No matter, this gorgeous, well-built woman with the cascading honey blond hair had never regretted her decision, not for a moment. Her instincts about Brandon Shaw had been right on, and her reward was a love unlike anything she had ever known or imagined.

Now, together, they stood as a unified team to fight the destruction of the world's jungles. Brandon Shaw, although not a scientist, was qualified to be here because of his life history, living in the jungle and witnessing first-hand what was happening there.

His mood became more somber, and it was not merely an act for his audience. "If you don't take action, those things you treasure so much; your favorite song, a poem, the feel of your loved one's fingers running through your hair, won't matter. And make no mistake; it isn't up to someone else. It's up to you! The biggest Achille's Heel of mankind is the belief that it always happens to someone else. Someone else will have to deal with 'it', whatever 'it' may be. Make no mistake. This time, the 'someone else', is you. You, me, and every person on this planet."

Then he visually scanned the audience. "Well, I see a few of you here today don't have any hair for your lover to run their fingers through, but you get my meaning!"

That simple line inspired a laugh from the crowd and changed the mood to a lighter tone. Brandon continued with his presentation for another fifteen minutes. By the time he reached the conclusion, he received a rousing ovation. Most of his audience even rose to their feet to show their enthusiasm as they clapped wildly.

Thirty minutes later, Brandon and Andrea with Naja at their side, stood at the exit door near the back of the meeting hall shaking hands with congratulators.

Andrea was also selling copies of a coffee table book she had put together containing some dialogue, but mostly pictures she had taken of the jungle, animals and Brandon in the jungle, in assorted situations, including some fascinating shots of The Lost City Of The Monkey God, with pyramids, stela and other stone monuments.

Appearing subtlety, in the line of greeters was a tall, thin, dark man, sporting a goatee wearing an expensive blue suit, and with his hair in dreadlocks. He eyed Brandon narrowly before approaching him. His hand was extended for a handshake, but his body language suggested something other than cordiality. Naja immediately sensed something, and issued a low growl, deep in her throat.

"Hello, Mista Shaw. How tings in Sambala?" the man said in a thick Jamaican accent.

Brandon eyed the man. "Sambala? Alright, I guess. Haven't been there in a while. Why do you ask?"

Brandon accepted the man's hand for a handshake.

"I jus wondering if you had seen Reggie Carlson lately?"

By now, other people were beginning to form a short queue, hoping to get a chance to meet Brandon Shaw and shake his hand.

Andrea, standing a few feet away heard the dark man's query and was suddenly on alert.

"Reggie Carlson?" Brandon said thoughtfully. "I know I've heard that name somewhere. I just can't quite..."

"He had a business dere. Not no mo."

Andrea quickly whispered in Brandon's ear. As she did so, Brandon's eyes narrowed.

He addressed the dark man again, but this time a lot more cautiously, and with a decidedly sterner tone, said, "I wouldn't call what he was running a business. More like a scam. Who are you and why do you ask?"

"I am his broder," came the reply.

"Aw yeah? Well, good luck with that. Reggie? Is that his name? Were you aware that he went around calling himself 'Smoke Jaguar'? An alias he bummed from an ancient Mayan King. A little presumptuous of him, don't you think? Anyway, if you've got something on your mind, step aside and wait until I'm through here. I've got other people to greet."

"No. I see you again. Maybe in Honduras."

"Whatever blows your skirt up," Brandon said in an obvious show of contempt, and dismissing the man. Then he turned his attention to other people who were waiting to meet him and either make comment or ask a question.

Three days later, as the passenger jet cruised at thirty thousand feet, headed south toward Honduras, Brandon casually commented to Andrea, "Something tells me we have not seen the last of the second Mister Carlson. My instinct tells me… trouble,"

Naja sat in a seat across the aisle from Brandon and Andrea. By paying enough to the right people, Naja was classified as a "service animal" on TACA Airlines.

Andrea listened to Brandon's admonition, but looked straight ahead and said nothing.

Then, Brandon Shaw began to smile broadly, grabbed Andrea's forearm and said, "I think I've got it! No, by Golly! I *KNOW* I've got it!"

Looking surprised at her man, Andrea asked, "Got what?"

Brandon laughed. "Sweetheart, Jungle Cargo is just fixing to go in a different direction, take on a whole new challenge, a whole new purpose, a whole new quest! Yes, by golly, this will be a whole new dynamic."

"Where you go, I will follow," Andrea said. "But where are we going?"

For the duration of the flight to La Ceiba, Honduras, Brandon explained in painful detail what his new plan for Jungle Cargo was to be. By the time the plane sat down, Andrea was so excited that she could hardly wait to get back to the compound and have a general meeting with the crew.

It was late afternoon by the time the duo had landed, cleared customs, then managed to catch a taxi to Cuyamel. So, there was no company meeting that evening. Just an announcement that there was *going to be* a meeting the following morning and a special note that everyone had better hold on to their hats for this one, that it would be nothing like the company had ever experienced before. Andrea ended her invitation by saying, "I promise!" Then smiled broadly.

CHAPTER TWO

A NEW DAWN AT JUNGLE CARGO

THE FOLLOWING MORNING WAS SATURDAY, AND IT BROKE early at Jungle Cargo. People began to gather just as the sun peeked over the horizon. The house girls, Anna Maria and Suyapa had been instructed that this was to be a particularly superb 'desayuno', and they were already bringing bowls of fresh fruit and other breakfast goodies to the long buffet tables. There was sliced papaya, mango, banana, pineapple and cantaloupe as well as wedges of orange and grapefruit. Then another bowl was filled with hard boiled eggs which seemed to be a favorite among the Jungle Cargo company.

In addition to the girls, also present were Lorenzo Ponce, a new employee named Adan, the company partner, Doug Bennett, friends from down the beach, Don Houseman and Mary, Brandon and Andrea and of course the jaguars. There was Naja, Cisco, and the two cubs, now called Naja II and Cisco Jr. Naja and Cisco laid contentedly on the deck, while the two cubs romped from one end of the broad deck to the other, playing like puppies.

Brandon and Andrea sat in chairs at the round metal table. The one with the brightly colored umbrella that advertised Cinzano. They were accompanied by Doug, Mary and Don.

Lorenzo was making do, sitting on a bench which ran along the deck railing. He was fussing over a bowl full of mango and papaya, squeezing lime juice on the fruit, while chatting with Adan.

There was anticipation in the air. Brandon had promised important news, and everyone wanted to hear what that news was, even Don and Mary, even though so far as they knew, whatever it was that Brandon had on his mind would not be affecting them.

Brandon would not disappoint. He finished speaking softly to Doug, then rose from his chair and walked to a spot by the deck railing. One last sip of rich, black coffee and he was ready to address the small congregation.

"May I have everyone's attention, please? Thank you. I would like to begin by saying that Andrea and I feel very honored to have all of you here by our side. We are a family. Andrea and I love you very much. That doesn't have anything to do with what I am about to say, but I felt I needed to say it anyway."

The response was a relaxed laughter.

"Jungle Cargo is about to undergo a dramatic change. Well, actually, a metamorphosis. It is a radical transition that represents the closing of one chapter, and an opening of a new one. It is, a new beginning, of sorts, whereby we give back, rather than just take from."

"What do you mean, Don Brandon?" Lorenzo asked.

"What I mean is this; I have never done one goddamn thing in my life for somebody else, or something else. Since the very beginning, the standard operating procedure around here has been to take from the jungle. Take from...

take from," Brandon pulled his hands toward his body to emphasize his meaning.

"There are only so many spoons full of sugar you can take from the sugar bowl before that bowl is empty. How many parrots can we remove from this jungle before there are no more parrots? How many parrots can be slaughtered by the fruit companies before there are no more parrots? Somebody has to step up and do something positive about it before the parrots are gone forever. You hear me? 'Forever' is a long time. When the parrots are gone, you can't just decide one day that you want a parrot and sew one together from cloth. Nobody else seems to give a damn, so, we are going to! This is a result of me listening to my own rhetoric. It seems like 'we' are always waiting for somebody else to step up and take responsibility, take action, to do something positive about any given situation.

"Well, 'we' can't wait any longer. It's up to us. Why? Because quite honestly, Jungle Cargo is guilty of being one of the biggest offenders. How many parrots have we removed from this jungle? How many coati mundis? How many monkeys? How many toucans? How many snakes? How many jaguarundis? Every one of those animals had a job to do in this jungle and we prevented them from doing it by removing them from the jungle and sending them thousands of miles away. In many cases, we sent them to their death. I knew it. I didn't give a fuck. Well now I care. I'm seeing things from a perspective I have never seen before."

"Jesus y Maria!" Lorenzo said softly.

Brandon looked at Lorenzo and shook his head. "Yes, Lorenzo. Jesus y Maria indeed! Hold on to your hats, because here is my plan. Jungle Cargo owns close to a thousand acres which surrounds this property. We own land to the left and right, but mostly going inland toward the main road. It's sitting there, dormant, doing nothing. It's covered in dense jungle and I've left it that way because it's the right thing to do. I've had several campocinos come to me wanting to do slash and burn farming, wanting to plant a corn milpa. I have told all of them no."

"Yeah," Lorenzo said, laughing. "I've been there when you told a couple of them. You said a lot more than just 'no'!"

"Damn!" Don said, jokingly. "And here I was, about to ask you if you'd like to build an RV park back there!"

Everyone laughed.

"I think not," Brandon said. "This grand plan unfolds in several phases. Phase one is *CONSTRUCTION*. We're going to build nice, wide, 'meandering' black top paths through that jungle. In multiple locations, there are going to be large, modern flight cages. Lots of them. There will also be what I want to refer to as 'support buildings' adjacent to each flight cage where food and cleaning supplies will be kept close at hand for workers. That way, a worker won't have to push some damned wagon or such along a winding path. What we're going to do is create an environment worthy of the finest zoo."

"Hijolé!" Lorenzo said. "That all sounds muy grandé, but what's it for, Jefe?"

"I knew you would ask," Brandon said with a smile. "Andrea is going to 'take the podium' now, so to speak. She will paint the colors into the picture for you." Brandon sat down and Andrea stood up to start speaking.

"Jungle Cargo is going to become a preserve, a conservatory. When we get licensed as such, we can do a lot of things that will benefit the psittacine birds of Honduras. This plan is multi-faceted and very complicated."

Andrea looked at Don Houseman. "Don, Jungle Cargo would like to offer you a job. Actually, several jobs."

"Doing what?" Don asked.

"Each year, untold thousands of parrots are shot to death by employees of fruit companies who are stationed in fields where produce is grown. They kill them because parrots, for instance, will fly into a field of watermelons and eat a hole the size of a silver dollar in every watermelon. Obviously, fruit growers can't afford that. So, they kill the parrots.

"What we want to hire you to do is, one; invent another way to repel parrots, to keep them away from the watermelon fields. There has to be a way. You have a very inventive mind. We think you would be the ideal person for the job. However, that job is down the road, because before that, we have a major undertaking for you. That is, if you want to accept the challenge."

Don looked non-plussed. "What challenge?"

Andrea smiled. "I'll get to it in a minute. I don't want to lose my place here. So, this is not all we are going to do. As a licensed preserve, we are going to hire lawyers to lobby in Tegusigalpa to make the killing of any kind of psittacine bird *against the law*. A crime punishable by a fine and jail time. Then of course there has to be a publicity campaign to get the word out, especially to the fruit companies and these Indians all over Honduras."

"That's it?" Lorenzo asked. "What about the path through the jungle and the flight cages, and, and the support structures? What's all of that?"

"Be patient, Lorenzo. I'm getting to that," Andrea said. Lorenzo raised his hands, palms upward and shrugged. "Intonces!" he commented.

Andrea laughed. "Lorenzo, it's going to be your job to fill every one of those flight cages with birds. But you must segregate. Put only yellow naped amazons in one cage, put blue crowned amazons in another cage, all by themselves.

Tovi parakeets go in another. Scarlet macaws go in another, etc."

"Ladies and gentlemen, for now we will continue to export a few, select parrots, but that faucet is going to be slowly closed because we are going to start breeding psittacines, raising our own parrots, exporting only birds that are born here at Jungle Cargo. But also, and most importantly, we will return a large percentage of the offspring into the wild. Instead of taking from the jungle, we are going to go in reverse and supply parrots to the jungle."

Lorenzo slowly stood up, as if he couldn't believe his ears. "Whaaat?"

"You heard me correctly," Andrea continued. "For years we have taken from the jungle. Now, Jungle Cargo is going to start returning animals to that jungle. We are going to give back, ladies and gentlemen.

"Within a short time, possibly as soon as a year, the only parrots we will export will be animals that were hatched right here at Jungle Cargo. We will not take from the jungle anymore, with one exception. We will 'borrow' breeding age birds. But those birds will never leave Honduras. They will simply add to our brood stock."

Then Andrea turned to Mary. "Mary, you seem perfectly happy in your retirement, taking care of Don and your new household. Lord knows, you deserve it after what you've been through. But if you want more, we can use your help."

"Doing what?" Mary asked.

"Oh my, you have so many talents. For one thing, we are going to need a top-notch nutritionist who can make sure every animal in our care is receiving the absolute best diet and food for their particular species."

Mary clapped her hands together involuntarily.

"Ooohh! I would love doing that, but I'm not sure I'm qualified."

"If you accept the position we have for you, we would fly in one of the top bird experts in the United States. He works for the San Antonio Zoo, in Texas. He would work with you for as long as it takes to train you and make you as skilled as he is. He would spend three months with you, if necessary."

Mary clasped her hands together again, and looked over at Don, seated next to her. "Would that be alright with you?"

"Of course," Don said. "I think it's exciting."

Andrea continued. "The fact is, we have jobs for everyone here, meaningful jobs, important jobs, and after the cages are constructed and we start filling them, we will be hiring more people. This is going to be a radical transformation. Jungle Cargo has never looked like this. With extra personnel, there will be more houses built on site."

"More houses?" Don said. "Well, that's my specialty. I've been a home builder all my life."

"Which brings us to the next subject that Andrea alluded to," Brandon interjected. "Before you start developing a gadget to scare away parrots from agricultural areas, we need you to design and build everything we've just mentioned, flight cages, support buildings, engineer the overall design, lay in the black-top paths. And that isn't all."

"My God," Don said, looking down and shaking his head. "I thought my usefulness to this world had, well… had come to a close. Now I find, my most glorious challenge may be ahead of me." The man was near tears. Mary reached out and took his hand.

The one person present who had not said anything was Doug Bennett. He stood apart, leaning against the deck railing, arms crossed and looking slightly in shock. This did not go unnoticed by Brandon or Andrea.

Brandon walked over to where Doug stood. Naja stayed close to her master, and the cubs followed, romping playfully in their youth.

"I know this comes as kind of a shocker," Brandon said softly to Doug. "But what it amounts to is this, you're going to have to work less for possibly a greater profit."

"How's that?" Doug asked.

"We're going to have to go up on the price of our livestock. And the price will be justified because a year from now, you'll be offering cage raised birds, exclusively. Nothing wild. The birds we offer will be so tame by the time they wind up in consumer's hands that no taming will be necessary, the way it is now. People won't be losing birds from some intestinal disease that quarantine didn't find. And we won't be losing them in quarantine to shock, which has always been a heart breaker.

"Plus, we're going to open this place up to the public and charge admission."

"That will spell disaster," Doug said, slightly alarmed.

"I know what you're thinking. But every guest who comes through here will be required to wear a face mask, and there will be no feeding of the animals."

"I need to think about it, but I'm uh, uh, still very hesitant."

"Well," Brandon said. "You're a partner, so naturally I am going to take your opinion into account. If you're against it, we won't do it. I was just looking at the extra revenue."

"How much uh, uh revenue are we talking about?"

"Well, it's like this, I'll get a couple of the radio DJs out here and feed 'em barbeque and booze, plus maybe throw in a hooker or two. I figure we'll get unlimited free advertising for a month following every time I do that. Bottom line, a couple of thousand per weekend."

Doug's eyes grew wide. "Dollars, or Limpiras?"

"Make that four thousand in Limpiras. A couple of thousand dollars."

"Per weekend?"

"Per weekend."

"Well, uh, uh, shit. I might have to reconsider my position."

"Oh no. I wouldn't want to try to influence your vote."

"Kiss my ass, Brandon Shaw!"

The two partners chuckled and turned their attention back to the other happenings on the deck. Naja had left Brandon's side, which was unusual, and walked over to Andrea, where the big cat was methodically sniffing the woman. Then suddenly, Naja raised up on her haunches, carefully placed her huge paws on Andrea's shoulders and began purring, then began rubbing her cheeks against Andrea's chest.

"What the hell?" Brandon said. "That's strange. What's going on? Are you wearing some kind of new perfume or something?"

"No," Andrea replied. "I don't know what's going on. Well, we'll talk later," she said, while trying to get Naja to take her paws off of her shoulders.

"Naja, get down," Brandon said. The jaguar responded to her master's voice immediately, carefully lowering her front half down onto the deck.

"I have never seen Naja do anything like that," Brandon said, slightly bemused. He looked at Andrea for some kind of an answer. "Want to give me a heads up about what I just saw here?"

"Well, I'm not sure. Not sure at all. But I think I might have an idea what it is. That is, what it might be."

Brandon looked at Andrea, then at Doug, and back to Andrea. Now he was confused. "Okay. You've got my attention. Pray tell, what's going on here?"

"Not now," Andrea stammered. "We've got too much on our plate already. And you just sprung this grand idea on me less than twenty-four hours ago. I'm still trying to process, absorb, wrap my head around the immensity of this project. It's exciting, but at this juncture, a little scary."

Brandon took a couple of steps closer to Andrea. Now, studying her expression intently, he said, "You're keeping something from me."

Andrea tried looking the other way, then back at Brandon. "It's nothing that won't keep. Let's get back to this meeting. There are people here wanting to know what's about to happen to their lives."

"Let them wait. There's plenty to eat." Then Brandon turned to face the present company. "Excuse Andrea and I for a minute, folks. We have to have a brief sub-meeting inside."

Then he turned back to Andrea, took her gently by the hand and led her through the patio doors to the inside of the house. Closing the door behind them, he turned to her and said, "Okay, what's going on? And no bullshit, I want the truth."

Andrea now led Brandon over to the sofa. "Sit down, Brandon."

Brandon sank down onto the sofa. "Oh shit! You're leaving me. Probably for that young umbrella salesman we saw working on the corner in La Ceiba."

"No. Besides, he's too short," Andrea said, a little exasperated. "Brandon, I'm late."

Brandon looked at her, puzzled. "Late for what? You're here. The meeting didn't start until…"

Andrea placed her finger over Brandon's lips. "Not that

kind of late. Uh, while we were in Atlanta, I noticed that I didn't start on time."

"Start on time?"

"Just hush and listen. You wanted me to tell you 'what's going on'. Well, this is what's going on. I didn't start on time. So, I went down to the hotel pharmacy and bought an EPT test kit."

"E-P-T? Every Person's… Talent? Temper? Tomato?"

"Shut up, Brandon. This is difficult enough, without you trivializing it."

"Okay, but what am I trivializing?"

"Dammit, Brandon, I'm pregnant."

"Well, okay, so you're pregnant. That doesn't mean that you… wait!" Brandon paused and his eyes grew wide. "Pregnant? Did you say pregnant? Did I just hear you say pregnant?"

"Yes, Brandon, pregnant."

Brandon stared at Andrea for a long moment. At first, he was silent. Then he got a far-away look in his eyes, but then he stood up and took Andrea into his arms and pulled her close.

"All my life, I've dreamed of having a son or daughter. But with my lifestyle I just dismissed it as out of reach. I had resigned myself to..."

"Brandon, get a grip. Tell me if you're happy about this or not."

"Happy? I've never been so happy in my entire life. I've got goosebumps all the way down to my toes. Can we share this with… them?" He gestured toward the gathering on the deck.

"If you wish. It's going to be kind of hard to keep it a secret for very long anyway."

Brandon hugged Andrea long and hard. "I want to thank you. But I'm at a loss for words. This is amazing. You are amazing. You and I are going to create a life? A human life?"

"Yes, we are," Andrea said with a smile and a sigh of relief. This because she had no idea how Brandon would react to the news. Her apprehension was the reason she hadn't told him before now. She was waiting for the right place, and the right moment. Now that she had told him, her insides were filled with love and happiness.

But there was little time to dwell on it, because Brandon had her by the hand and was leading her back through the patio doors, out onto the deck.

Once there, he proudly (and very loudly) proclaimed, "Everybody! I want your attention, please. Andrea has just told me that I am about to become a father."

Everyone cheered. Then he added, "Oh, by the way, Andrea is also going to be a mother… the mother… of our child, which she is carrying inside of her… now. *Right now!* Child. Our child!" Everyone laughed, then clapped at Brandon's uncontrollable joy.

Then he added, "And Naja knew. Can't fool a jaguar." He called Naja to him, leaned down and talked to her as he scratched her behind the ears. "You knew, huh, girl?"

Yes, Andrea thought. Naja knew. But then, what else does Naja know?

Brandon then asked for Lorenzo's help in arranging for a celebration to mark this most special day. Food, music, people.

Lorenzo responded by saying, "You talking about my specialty, Jefe. I'm going to put a pinché party together for you. We going to celebrate all sorts of things tonight. You becoming a daddy. Hijolé! That just blows my mind. We going to celebrate the new Jungle Cargo. We going to do it in style. I got carte blanche?"

"You've got carte blanche," Brandon said with a huge, broad smile.

Lorenzo went to Andrea and took her in his arms. "Forgive me. I know I never hugged you before. But I got to hug you now. You're going to be a mommy. And me, I'm going to be, well, I'm going to be Uncle Lorenzo."

"Yes, you most certainly are," Andrea said as she returned Lorenzo's hug. People began lining up to congratulate Andrea, first, and then Brandon. Meanwhile, Lorenzo cornered Suyapa and Anna Maria, and gave them instructions about the fiesta which they only had one day, this day, to prepare for. There would be a mountain of things to do. And Lorenzo was honored to do them. He couldn't remember having been this excited in a long time.

"*Uncle Lorenzo!*" he said loudly, with pride, to the world in general. "Pinché, Tio Lorenzo!" Then he laughed as he tromped down the steps to climb into the Jeep and head to town for supplies.

CHAPTER THREE

The Fiesta

FELIZADADES A LOS DOS POR SU EMBARAZO! That's what the twenty-foot-long banner said. Lorenzo had managed to find somebody to make it. Then he strung it up between two coconut palms. Translated: CONGRATULATIONS TO YOU BOTH ON THE PREGNANCY!

Brandon and Andrea stood at the deck railing looking out at the bright blue and white banner in mild shock and awe, but also with pleasure and grateful for what Lorenzo had managed to pull together in record time.

Looking at the banner, Andrea said, "Well, if there is anybody within twenty miles of here that didn't get the message, they certainly know it now."

"I wonder how he got that done so fast?" Brandon said. "Hell, I wonder how he got *everything* done so fast!"

"I don't know," Andrea said with a smile. "But when Lorenzo gets inspired, there is nothing that will stop him."

It wasn't long before the party was in full swing. It seemed like Lorenzo had invited half of La Ceiba, not the least of which was Brandon's banker and his family. There were a lot of people, but they were spread out all over the property; some were up on the deck where the goodies were being served, some people were out in the yard, chatting it up. Some were on the beach in front of the house.

New arrivals all made their way up onto the deck where they were greeted by Brandon, Andrea, and Naja. Then guests offered their congratulations before being offered drinks, prepared by a bartender that Lorenzo had miraculously come up with.

Leticia, Lorenzo's new girlfriend, was also in attendance. She offered her services to Andrea, saying that while she was not a doctor, she could certainly give intermediary check-ups between Andrea's doctor's visits and perhaps save her an occasional trip into town when she needed something. She also volunteered to find the very best 'gyno' for Andrea, an offer that Andrea gladly accepted.

Smoke curled upward from a large fire pit prepared by a ranch cocinero who Lorenzo had contacted to handle the cooking of several meats. But as it turned out, most of the meat was spiny lobsters. After all, it was lobster season and Lorenzo had somehow found the time to go to Sambala and alert every lobster fisherman in sight that Don Brandon needed lobsters for a fiesta.

So, periodically, Sambala lobster fishermen would pull up on the beach in front of Jungle Cargo with their cayuco canoes and offload up to a dozen lobsters weighing three pounds to five pounds each. By the time things slowed down, Lorenzo had between fifty and sixty large lobsters for the cook to add to the grill. When the lobsters were cooked, a cook's assistant would bring them up the stairs to a serving area on the deck. Several side dishes were offered to compliment the lobsters including a scrumptious mango salsa, fried platanos, and a type of spicy rice, plus guacamole.

Dining was informal. People would eat when they were hungry by selecting what they wanted from bowls and platters placed on a long table, dressed with a white table cloth.

The party was going well, not too sedate, not too rowdy. The atmosphere was respectful and mindful of the purpose for this celebration.

At one point, Andrea turned to Brandon and said softly, "And to think, I was worried about how you would take the news."

"I'm the happiest man in the world," he said, as he put another spoon full of mango ice cream in his mouth. "I don't care if it's a boy or a girl. I just want to hear it call me Daddy!"

Andrea smiled, and laughed her signature lilting laugh.

Brandon continued. "It's like a miracle."

"It is a miracle," Andrea said. "All children are miracles."

Lorenzo had his boom box plugged in somewhere downstairs in the carport, and reasonably good music was playing. But suddenly there was an interruption, a disturbance from somewhere on the beach to the right of the house. Lorenzo hollered from downstairs, saying that Brandon and Andrea needed to come down to the front yard. Concerned about what was going on, the duo went cautiously down the stairs to respond to whatever it was.

A contingent of dancers from Sambala, dressed in costumes that hinted strongly of African heritage, appeared on the beach, walking together, then turned left and made their way into the yard. Their costumes involved a lot of large feathers and body paint. Altogether, there were close to forty of them. Seeing Brandon and Andrea standing close to the bottom landing of the steps, a spokesman stepped forward.

He addressed the two people in a loud enough voice for everyone to hear, and indeed, the party guests were gathered to see what the dancers were going to perform.

In his very best Garifuna/Spanish, he said, "Don Brandon and Doña Andrea, we hear the good news. We come here to show respect, and to entertain for you."

Then he took three steps back and the performance began with the thundering, hypnotic rhythm of multiple drums. The dancers formed into a pattern and began moving to the rhythm of the drums. In the beginning of the dance, the performers took two sideways steps to their left, then back. They turned a 360-degree circle and repeated. At one point, they all extended their arms and yelled, "Huh!" then swooped and swirled.

Andrea remembered another time when these very same dancers appeared between the house and the compound to honor Brandon for ridding them of the voodoo priest, Smoke Jaguar. That dance had been an artistic interpretation of events and had been disturbing because it had somehow depicted Brandon of possibly morphing into a jaguar. It had shaken Andrea, but later she dismissed it as nothing more than a folk tale put to dance. Even so, she had never been able to forget it.

But now, in this dance, a dancer appeared, wearing a wooden mask depicting the shape of a jaguar's head, but painted black. This was obviously Naja. Pseudo Naja danced between two other dancers that were apparently meant to represent Brandon and Andrea. That was kind of nice, and Andrea smiled.

Then suddenly, a smaller dancer appeared from somewhere, a half-sized dancer and this one carried with him a wooden carving of a jaguar mask in his hands. In the performance, the small dancer would periodically hold the jaguar mask up, in front of his face for several moments while spinning around multiple times, then he would remove the mask.

This upset Andrea greatly. As she watched, she said to Brandon through clenched teeth, "What the living hell is that supposed to translate to?"

"I don't know," Brandon said defensively. "They're north coast people of African heritage. Their whole culture is driven by folklore."

"Yeah," Andrea said, near tears. "Lots of goddamn folklore!" She turned and rushed up the steps, dashed across the deck, through the patio doors and into the house, closing the patio doors hard behind her.

Brandon wanted to be polite and stay until the dance came to an end, but he knew that Andrea was experiencing some kind of an emotional meltdown, and he felt he had to go to her. So, he motioned to the dancers, thanking them, then asked them to stay and enjoy the party, to eat and have drinks. Then he dashed up the stairs to comfort his woman. Inside the house, he found Andrea sitting on the sofa, dabbing at tears with a tissue. He sank down on his knees in front of her.

"I'm here," he said. "I'm trying to understand what it is you're so upset about."

"Don't give me that horseshit," she said through sniffles. "You know exactly what I am upset about. I want this to be a normal baby. Not some hangover from a two-thousand-year-old aberration with a head like a jaguar."

"Oh, for crying out loud!" Brandon said, as he rose and went to the fridge for a beer. "It's going to be a normal baby."

"Well what about that dancer?" Andrea almost wailed, waving her hand toward the front yard.

Brandon rolled his eyes. "Fuck that goddamned dancer! What do you think those people are, seers into the future? They're a bunch of kids with vivid imaginations and a lot of time on their hands. There isn't a lot to do in a village like Sambala except sit around and think up bullshit to make life a little less boring. 'The Strip' in Sambala consists of one trucha."

Andrea started to calm down. "You really think so?"

"Yeah," Brandon said vigorously. "I really do think so. I'll tell you something else that I think. I think your body is going through some pretty wild hormonal changes right now. I mean, I've never been through this with a woman, but Doug has, and he told me how his wife was bouncing off the walls when she was knocked up."

"Brandon!"

"What?... Oh, sorry. I mean, pregnant."

"Thank you."

"Anyway, all that was out there was dinner and a show. Those kids didn't mean anything by what they were doing. They damn sure didn't mean to upset you. They were just adding spice to the lobsters. Showing respect. We should be honored."

Andrea thought for a long minute. "Okay, I guess you're right. It's just been a very busy, very emotional day. I over-reacted."

Brandon pulled her to her feet and put his arms around her. Just then, the patio doors opened, and Mary stepped inside.

"Everything alright in here?" Mary asked.

"Yeah," Brandon said with a smile. "She's just a little tired and emotional."

"Well, hey!" Mary said. "It's to be expected. After all, she is knocked up!"

CHAPTER FOUR

The Planning

The party had been a tremendous success, despite the emotional overload that Andrea had experienced. After thinking about it, she realized that Brandon was right. The performers were young people from Sambala whose heads were filled with folk tales and imagination. Actually, they were showing strong imaginations and story building skills by creating such a dance.

Now, with that landmark celebration behind them, serious planning of Brandon's grand dream was taking place. And if it sounded great when they talked about it on the front deck, seeing it take shape on paper was almost overwhelming. Brandon, Doug, Andrea and Don Houseman spent hours at the dining-room table discussing every finite detail. Even Lorenzo occasionally joined them to lend input. His opinions were valuable. After all, he saw things from the mechanic's point of view. Concept was one thing, but how would something work from an actual hands-on standpoint? Therein was crystal clear truth.

One place where they kept hitting a snag was in the actual lay-out of the path and close at hand flight cages.

The topography of the landscape behind the Jungle Cargo compound was to some degree unknown because of the tangled jungle growth.

At one point, Brandon threw down his pencil and said with frustration, "You know what? We need Bruce Burns!"

Doug looked at Brandon, slightly confused. "Uh, Bruce Burns? Who is that?"

Brandon then related the story of the search for Naja. "… So, then a guy that had been sitting there, in the Jungle Inn restaurant the whole time, introduces himself. He said his name was Bruce Burns and that he had just finished mapping the entire site at the Lost City, 'by air'. I thought he was talking about doing something from a chopper, but he wasn't. Turns out he is a drone pilot. To make a long story short, he gets this metal box from his Jeep and pulls out this strange looking gizmo with four propellers, all pointed upward. You ever seen a drone?"

Don and Doug both nodded their heads. "Of course."

"Well, I hadn't," Brandon said with a hint of defensiveness. "Guess I've spent too much time in this frapping jungle. Anyway, he volunteers his services. The next thing I know, we're looking at every square inch of the jungle from an angle that would have otherwise been impossible. It was… well, a lifesaver. Within a little while, we spotted Naja. I had been going through that frigging tangle for three days, *in the rain* looking for her without success. It's a miracle that I didn't get pneumonia.

"Anyway, if we could get Bruce Burns to come here with his drone, I have the feeling he could eliminate a whole bird's nest of problems by sky mapping the entire property for us."

"What an excellent idea," Don said. "Just excellent! Do you think you can get him on the phone?"

"Let's find out," Brandon said, and picked up his cell

phone from the table. "I put his number in this thing when we were at the Jungle Inn. Now I'm glad I did!"

He found the contact, pressed the proper buttons and within a few seconds, Bruce Burns answered the phone.

"Hello?"

"Bruce?"

Slight pause. "Brandon? Brandon Shaw?"

"Yep, it's me."

"Well, as I live and breathe! How are you?"

"Fine as frog hair. How about you?"

"Oh, same as always. Couldn't be better. How are Naja and Cisco?"

"Ohhh, have I got some news for you! The answer is, they are both fine. But..."

"Don't do that to me. I know how loaded your 'buts' can be."

"Well, it seems there was a little hanky-panky going on in that jungle between the two afore mentioned creatures."

"Don't tell me!"

"Bruce, there are now two little jaguars that are duplicates of their parents. A male that is a carbon copy of Cisco, a female that is another Naja."

"Oh my God! Oh my God! I have got to see them. Can you send me a picture?"

"Yeah, but I don't think that is good enough."

"What do you mean?"

"Bruce, I need you and your drone. Can you come down here?"

"Nothing on this earth could stop me."

"Good. I'll explain everything when you get here. There will be a ticket waiting for you when you get to the airport. When you get here, you will be our guest, so no hotel."

"We have a guest room that needs to be broken in," Don Houseman said. "He can stay with us."

"I can hardly contain my excitement," Bruce said. "I'm bringing a couple of cameras. I want to get a whole album of photos. Naja and Cisco, parents! I can hardly believe it!"

Brandon handed the phone to Andrea who would handle details of the flight. She talked with Bruce Burns for a couple of minutes, then ended the call.

"That is a smart move," she said. "It'll be good to see Bruce again too."

"He sure saved our chops in the Mosquitia," Brandon said. "I'm not sure how that story would have played out without his help."

Andrea agreed, then phoned the travel agent to make arrangements for the first flight from Tampa to Honduras.

When Bruce Burns arrived at the house at Jungle Cargo, he had barely greeted everybody and hugged them before he looked through the patio doors and spotted Naja and the cubs. Abandoning ceremony, he dashed outside to say hello to Naja and meet the cubs.

The man expressed his glee with sounds of laughter, on his knees, talking with the cubs as he rubbed their ears and petted them. Here was a genuinely happy man who wanted nothing more at the moment than to be with the trio of jaguars. It was a tropical Norman Rockwell scene.

Eventually, he came back into the house to retrieve two cameras that he had brought with him for the purpose of photographing the cats. Then, he spent the next hour taking hundreds of pictures from a myriad of angles as he continued to laugh and play with them.

The cubs were perfect photography subjects because

nothing was going to interfere with their romping play. Their antics were delightful, and now, recorded. Naja was the perfect, sedate mother who allowed herself to be used as a combination playground and jungle gym. But the cubs were growing larger, weighing at least fifty pounds each. Their climbing all over her was bound to be slightly painful. To look in her proud face however, one would never know it. It didn't take an animal psychologist to see the love and pride in her eyes.

At last, jaguar time wound down and Bruce was ready to come inside to meet with 'the humans' and find out why he was here.

"Oh my!" Bruce said as he settled into a chair at the dining room table, which had become the makeshift conference table. "Those cubs are amazing. And lucky. Lucky that is, to be raised here, out of danger, surrounded by love, good nutrition, medical care should they need it. The jungle isn't getting any easier these days."

"No, it isn't," Brandon agreed. "You know, Bruce, it's funny you should say that because in a way, that's why we're at this crossroads, and, it's the reason you're here."

So it was that Brandon began to detail a full, three-dimensional explanation of what was on his mind. As he talked, other members of the company managed to arrive and join Bruce, Andrea and Brandon at the table.

The longer Brandon talked, the more enthusiastic and excited he became. Andrea looked at him a little surprised but pleased to see some enthusiasm in this man who rarely displayed that emotion.

He used a piece of large drafting paper to make a rough sketch, showing the trail he had in mind, a bird's eye view of the flight cage positions with support buildings. But there was more. A lot more. Now, Brandon added small, one room cabins toward the back of the property, and most surprising of all, another house, much larger than the house they were currently in, to be built less than a hundred yards farther down the beach, to the west of the house they were in. In other words, the opposite direction from Sambala.

This came as a complete surprise to Andrea. "What is this house? Who will live there?"

"We will!" Brandon said.

"What?

"Well, there's a couple of considerations. Technically, I gave this house to Lorenzo and the girls when we thought we were going to live in Florida. I even legally deeded it over to them. So, it's not right that we should just all of a sudden show up again and take the house over. That's number one. Then too, we're going to need more room. We've got to have a nursery for Little Brandon."

"Wait!" Bruce said. "Is there something I'm missing here? Did I just hear Brandon say that you are going to have a baby?" His mouth fell open.

"Yes," Andrea said with a smile.

"Oh my God!" Bruce said, as he rose from his chair to hug Andrea. "I'm going to hit emotional overload here. First, it's these precious jaguar cubs… and now this! I'm dizzy. I need to sit down for a minute. When did you find out about this?"

"I took a test when we were in Atlanta the other day."

"This is so exciting!"

"Yes, it is," Brandon said. "And that is the reason for a lot of things including the new house with a nursery and a much-much larger deck. But the new deck railing has to be built with babies in mind. That means installing either galvanized hog wire along the railings, or pickets that are no more than six inches apart. Air flow is always a consideration in this Honduras heat. So, I'm leaning toward the hog wire. But, you see, my life has changed in the past year or so. What I mean by that is, now I have to get that woman over there with the long blond hair to give input since she's going to be living there too."

"That's considerate of you," Bruce said. "Also, might keep you from getting hit over the head. I know in my house, the two magic words are, 'Yes Dear!'"

"Yeah, I thought making the adjustment was going to be hard, kind of like giving up part of my power or some stupid bullshit thing. But it's not like that at all. Actually, it's kind of fun."

Andrea moved to where Brandon was sitting and cuddled against him, so that he could put his arm around her.

"My, my, my!" Bruce said, shaking his head. "Chivalry comes to the jungle. Well, by God! It's a beautiful thing! Okay, where do we start on this project? Obviously, I'm here to do aerial mapping."

In less than an hour, the group had assembled on the deck, beneath a 12' X 12' "easy up" shelter that Bruce had brought with him. It was a great help to shade him and the other viewers who wanted to watch the drone in flight. A shaded area made it much easier to see the screen of the tablet, but it also provided welcome shade without obstructing any breeze.

Now, with a soft whirr, the drone lifted off from the deck and flew quickly skyward. Even as the instrument flew, Bruce was inputting information into a computer which was also tied to the drone. The data was instructing the drone to map the complete area Brandon had described. It would fly back and forth in an overlay pattern.

"So, how much territory do you have here, Brandon?"

"Five hundred hectares."

"Wait a minute! I thought you said you have a thousand acres."

"Yeah, so?"

"Well a hectare is something like 2.47 acres. If you have five hundred hectares, you have closer to.... One thousand, two hundred and thirty-five acres. I think. That's in my head. I'd have to get a calculator to make sure, but I know I'm close."

"So, I have over two hundred more acres than I thought I did. That's nice."

According to Brandon, the property was a rough rectangle, with about two thousand yards beachfront, then going back into the jungle, toward the main road in parallel property lines. In fact, a satellite map showed the property lines precisely by using a special 'app' that Bruce had in his computer. So, Bruce programmed Snoopy (his drone) to do an overlay map of the entire area shown on the satellite map. After adjustments press a few buttons, and Snoopy was on his way. The drone would even remember where it left off when it came in for battery replacements.

Everybody was transfixed on the tablet screen, watching as the miniature aircraft flew over their home area and showed them their world from an entirely different view from what they were accustomed. Although fascinating, everything was routine for the first half hour. Then Brandon spotted something in the middle of the thick part of the jungle that caught his eye.

"Wait! What the hell is that?" He pointed to a green cluster that looked like it was a planted crop, with a small building on one side.

"I see it too," Andrea said.

Bruce put the drone in reverse and backed up to the questionable location. Then he hovered while they examined the thing they were looking at. Bruce zoomed in tighter.

"Sonofabitch!" Brandon said. "Somebody is growing weed on my property. Look there! They've even built some kind of a shelter. The bastards are camping right here on my property and growing weed. Dirty bastards!"

"You want me to take care of it?" Andrea asked.

"Ohhh yeah! I think you'd better," Brandon answered.

Bruce looked up, first at Andrea, then at Brandon. "What's going on?"

"Long story," Brandon said with a smile. "Andrea used to be a fed. You might say, that's how we met."

"Yes, you might say that," Andrea said coyly.

"That's just *got to be* a fascinating story," Bruce said, turning his attention back to the screen.

Andrea picked up the phone and made a call. She then instructed Bruce what email to transmit his 'evidence footage' to.

"I'm gonna love this," Brandon said.

Within an hour, a helicopter appeared over the suspicious area and began to circle. Bruce still had the drone in the air but flying at a much lower elevation than the chopper.

Three 'drogeros' appeared from under the makeshift shelter and started looking up at the helicopter, pointing. They appeared excited, but there was little they could do except to run, which they apparently decided to do. They disappeared back under the makeshift shelter for a few moments, long enough to grab whatever they couldn't do without. Then they began running down a trail, which was hard to follow with the drone because it was beneath the jungle canopy. Even so, Bruce managed to get enough glimpses of them that he could follow them and keep the drone hovering over them.

Andrea transmitted their escape to whoever she was talking to. They already had forces on the ground and were waiting for the three drogeros near the road. The three criminals ran headlong into the arms of Honduran authorities, who immediately took them into custody and slapped handcuffs on them.

Meanwhile, another team of drug officers repelled down lines to the ground at the site of the marijuana field, and the marijuana plants were destroyed, as well as the makeshift shelter. After that, the chopper retrieved the crew and was gone as quickly as it had arrived.

"And that is how you do that!" Andrea said with satisfaction. Everyone applauded.

The aerial mapping continued as if there had been no interruption. Brandon watched the screen intently, learning things about his property that he had never known, or for that matter, cared about, until now.

Once the aerial mapping was completed, Bruce printed the entire topography grid on oversized pieces of paper that could be fitted together. When done, the map covered the entire dining room table. It was at this point that Don Houseman more or less took over. He mapped out the best trail based on the topography. Brandon stood to one side of him, Andrea on the other. Doug and Lorenzo filled in the opposite side of the table.

Meanwhile, Bruce had done his job, so he mixed a cocktail and wandered out onto the deck to enjoy it and play with the jaguars. But a few minutes later, he opened one of the patio doors and said, "There's a rather odd-looking gentleman standing in your front yard, just looking up at the deck. I think you should come see."

Everyone immediately abandoned what they were doing at the dining-room table and went outside to the deck railing to look down, toward the beach and see who the person was.

Brandon wasn't sure, but thought he recognized the man. "Oh! Isn't that whatizname, who came to the presentation in Atlanta?"

"Reggie's brother," Andrea said, staring down at the figure who stood in the yard, now staring up at Brandon.

"I didn't recognize him at first because he isn't wearing that suit anymore."

"No," Andrea said. "More like, 'Sambala couture'!" She said it with a hint of sarcasm in her voice.

Brandon raised his voice loud enough for Reggie's brother to hear. "Is there something on your mind?"

"I jus wan to see where de great Brandon Shaw live."

"Well, now you've seen. Unless there's something I can do for you, I suggest you stroll on down the beach. Hey! What the fuck is your name, anyway?"

"Oswald. You know, like Lee Harvey, de assassin."

With that, Brandon turned and headed for the stairs. But Oswald Carlson took Brandon's suggestion and left the premises at a somewhat hastened pace.

Meanwhile, Naja had picked up on Brandon's anger and went down the steps at lightning speed. Brandon saw what was happening just in time.

"Oh shit! Naja! Ka-nu!"

Naja had almost reached Oswald Carlson but put on the brakes at the sound of her master's command. Instead, she issued a thunderous roar. Oswald Carlson hadn't realized Naja was behind him, so when he heard the deafening roar within a few feet of him, the reaction was immediate and almost comical. Oswald lost control of his bowels, fouling himself, and then fled down the beach, stumbling and falling several times as he went.

Naja returned to the deck with a satisfied expression on her face.

Brandon said, "We're going to have trouble with that asshole."

"Perhaps," Andrea quipped. "But first, he may need to change his pants!"

Everyone laughed, then, returned inside the house to continue planning of The New Jungle Cargo.

CHAPTER FIVE

Planning an Ideal

LORENZO STOOD, LEANING AGAINST THE DECK RAILING, sipping his coffee. Close at his side sat Cisco, the male jaguar that Naja had encountered in the Mosquitia jungle when she was fleeing from the highly inebriated archaeologist who had taken a pot-shot at her. Subsequent to that encounter, Cisco had become the father of Naja's cubs and was adopted into the Brandon Shaw family of people and critters.

Here was a wild, jungle denizen who had been immediately tamed so that he could blend into this environment. It happened because of the incredible ability Brandon Shaw had for communicating with animals, and jaguars in particular. But it was Lorenzo that Cisco had decided to cleave to. This was based on the mysterious decision-making process known only to jungle animals.

For now, Cisco was enjoying the fruit of his loins. His two cubs played happily with their father, giving Naja a temporary respite. The two cubs launched mock attacks against each other, using their dad as home base. This was interspersed between occasional short races across the deck as first, the female cub chased the rosetted brother. Then roles would be reversed.

Lorenzo spent the time between sips of coffee silently watching the antics around him. It was early morning, and the most treasured of daily rituals was in progress.

Anna Maria and Suyapa placed bowls of tropical fruit on the long table, along with a bowl of hard-boiled eggs. There were also fresh tortillas, heated and placed inside a tortilla warmer.

As always, everyone was automatically invited to partake of the repast. This morning was a little busier than usual, albeit the focus was shifted drastically from the normal day's compound activities. Planning of the new Jungle Cargo had gone deep into the night, but a basic layout had been completed and now Brandon wanted to waste no time in putting the plan into motion.

The rough drawings would probably be sufficient for permit acquisition. The main drawings the Atlantida bureaucrats would be interested in were the drawings on large denomination Limpira bills, the grease which kept bureaucrats in Honduras well oiled.

Next, Don would need blueprints. There was no time to mess around. He put in a phone call to a couple of people he had worked with in the states. Luckily, with modern communications, he would be able to email details of the plans to them to work from. This would save time and the expense of flying them from Honduras, then flying the completed plans back to Honduras.

Don would also need a very large crew of carpenters, all of which were experienced and knew what they were doing. That probably wasn't going to be easy to accomplish. A lot of interviewing had to be done to weed out the amateurs, and most of all, persons of low moral character. Brandon had made it clear that he would tolerate no debauchery of any kind on the property. Topping that list was drunkenness and theft. So, whoever was hired to work within the Jungle Cargo environ had to be of good moral character.

Without waiting for the architects to complete their blueprints, an ad was placed in the local *LA PRENSA* newspaper announcing a search for qualified carpenters. The ad was very specific about skill qualifications and advised that all applicants must pass a background check, and a drug test. That part would take care of a lot of the 'weeding out'!

Then, of course, a sit down pow-wow was scheduled with Brandon's banker. Rumors had already reached the esteemed Mr. Almendarez. After all, Lorenzo had seen to it that the gentleman and his family had been invited to the 'pregnancy announcement party'.

With Andrea at his elbow, and frequently whispering advice in his ear, Brandon was lining everything out as if he had done this many times before, which of course he had not. Don Houseman also had a tremendous amount of input. All this was concerning the new construction. As for the operations of the new Jungle Cargo, that planning was placed in the capable hands of Doug Bennett and Lorenzo. Together, they were mapping out an entire pro-forma.

Plans eventually grew to include a small, one thousand square foot office. After all, one could not expect all sorts of people to come tromping in and out of a residence. Besides, there would be the need for office machines, file cabinets, a genuine conference table, etc.

It was an ambitious plan. But with the experience and expertise of Don Houseman, things were moving along like a well-oiled machine. However, no matter how involved the team became in minutia, Brandon never strayed too far from his plans for a new home for himself, Andrea and the new member of the family. It was clear he would be a doting father.

Andrea was mildly surprised at seeing this side of the jungle man, but she was also very pleased. A few days ago, she had been apprehensive about being pregnant. Now, she was the happiest woman in the world.

At the end of a very long Tuesday, everyone broke up the huddle and went their respective ways to rest and regroup. Even the girls, Anna Maria and Suyapa, left to go visit their families in Sambala. This left Brandon and Andrea alone for the evening, something that had become a rarity of late. Andrea did not miss the opportunity to strip Brandon of his clothes and pull him into the shower.

"I've discovered something about pregnant women," she said, with a coy smile.

"Yeah? What's that?" Brandon responded.

"We're so horny that we just want to eat you up!"

With that, she placed her arms around Brandon's neck and pulled him down to her where her mouth met his in a long, deeply passionate kiss. Feeling her full breasts against his chest triggered everything in Brandon that Andrea desired. And that was just the beginning. Her kisses and touches found their way to other parts of his body. Despite his fatigue, it didn't take Brandon long to respond. He had been hungry for his woman, but there was always something in the way, just one more thing to do. And that one more thing always somehow managed to become two, then three.

But now, in this moment, Andrea was taking charge and she was not going to allow anything in the world to be 'just one more thing' before she became one with the man she loved. Now, more deeply than ever.

In the shower, she straddled Brandon's muscular body and absorbed him into herself. The moment was tender and sweetly passionate, filled with love and the sounds of love. But that was only the beginning. After they had finally managed to finish their shower, Andrea dragged Brandon into the bedroom and over the next several hours, showed him just how much hunger she had for him. Dawn found them peacefully asleep, wrapped in each other's arms.

On Wednesday morning, the fresh air blew down from the mountainside behind Jungle Cargo. A tropical rain was coming. You could smell it in the air. It smelled fresh and clean. The strong breeze blew the coconut palm fronds around. This was quickly joined by the distant sound of thunder. Then came the rain, lightly pattering on the roof and walls at first, then it came down harder. It was perfect weather for deep, restful sleep. And to that end, Andrea pressed herself even tighter against Brandon.

Out on the deck, beneath the extended overhang of the roof, Naja and her cubs looked out at the beautiful rain as it pattered against the small waves of the Caribbean in front of the house. This was the ideal Cuyamel. Beautiful, tranquil, peaceful, idealistic.

It was the Cuyamel that Lorenzo worried would be lost if Brandon turned this near sacred place into a public arena. He didn't like the idea, and he knew that Doug Bennett felt the same way, although Señor Doug was being swayed by the potential for large amounts of revenue.

As Lorenzo sat in the carport beneath the house, drinking morning coffee, Cisco at his side, he pondered his worry. In this moment of reverie, he also stared out at the crystal blue waters as the rain pattered down. The more he thought about it, the more he knew he must speak his heart and tell Don Brandon Shaw what was bothering him.

"Do not turn Cuyamel into a tourist attraction," he would say. "To do so will be to completely destroy this magical place. You will take away something that can never be returned." Yes, goddammit! He would say that to the jefe because he knew he must. He just hoped that Don Brandon would be receptive and listen. Better yet, he hoped Don Brandon would understand his concerns.

Lorenzo had made an important decision and he felt good about it. He knew it was the right thing to do. *You know, he* thought to himself, *Sometimes things just can't be about money. Other things are more important.*

It was almost mid-morning before the rain let up. Brandon and Andrea timed rising from their restful sleep with the end of the rain. This morning was different from the norm. There was no early morning get together on the front deck with an informal mapping out of the day. No bowls of fresh, tropical, fruit, pan dulce and hard-boiled eggs.

Instead, it was a slow awakening. Brandon and Andrea filled their coffee cups and wandered out onto the deck where they plopped down in lounge chairs. Naja and her cubs were there to greet the duo. Taking their cue from their mother, the cubs were learning that it was the right thing to do to go to Brandon and Andrea and rub against them like house cats. It was the jaguar way of letting these humans know, all was well in this, their home. The humans normally reciprocated by scratching them behind the ears and petting them. All was as it should be. It was a good morning.

"How's that baby?" Brandon asked Andrea, over his coffee, as he scratched Baby Naja's head.

"Fine."

"We're going to have to make an appointment with a baby doctor right away."

"Actually, Leticia said she was going to handle that for

me. She's going to check and see who the most respected person around La Ceiba is, and then call me."

"Leticia? Lorenzo's Leticia?"

"Yeah. She's a nurse and knows just about everybody."

"Oh. Well I think that's wonderful. I appreciate her help. She and Lorenzo are getting pretty thick, huh?"

"It appears that way. She's a good person. I'm happy for Lorenzo."

"You think they'll, uh…"

"Most likely."

Brandon thought for a moment. "Lorenzo, married! Good grief! Now there's an image."

"Ah! He'll take to it like a duck to water."

"Hmm. Maybe. One way or the other, it'll be good for him." Brandon paused for a minute. Then, "Andrea, I only have one concern about a baby coming into our lives."

"What's that, Sweetie?"

"This may sound strange. Even a bit selfish. But, please, don't ever let the romance go out of our romance."

Andrea smiled. "You have my word," she said as she reached across to take Brandon's hand. "I know what you're talking about. I've seen it a hundred times. I'm not going to let it happen to us."

It would be easy in one way, she thought. *But not so easy* in another way. Brandon seemed like a man driven with this new quest of his. And she wasn't sure if it was a mission inspired by a desire, or one driven by guilt. Maybe it wasn't important, if the outcome would be the same. In either case, she supported his overall goal. Aside from that, she was gladdened and admittedly, a bit surprised by his overwhelming acceptance of approaching fatherhood.

"Those blue eyes never looked so blue, or so beautiful before," she heard someone say. It was Brandon. She had allowed her thoughts to carry her far away.

"Oh! Thank you. I'm glad you think so," she answered. But something was on her mind. No, something was distracting her. The two jaguar cubs, now close to eight months old, were behaving strangely. Though large, well over fifty pounds, they were still considered cubs and would be until they were a year old. But their behavior in this moment was not 'cub like.'

At first, something drew them to her, and they began sniffing her very closely. This continued for a full minute at least. Then, they flanked her as she sat in the chaise lounge. Little Cisco took up a position on her left side, while Little Naja duplicated Cisco's actions, on her right side. They sat on their haunches and looked ahead, alert, as if guarding her. All kitten-like play had vanished. These animals were serious.

"What's going on, Brandon?" she asked, nervously.

"I'm not sure," he replied while watching the cubs' business-like mannerisms. "But my suspicion is, they know you are pregnant, and they are protecting you."

"Really?" she said, looking back and forth at each cub. "I'm not sure how I feel about this."

"Well, I don't know how you feel about it, but if I were you, I think I would just try to get used to it because if my guess is right, you have two bodyguards that are going to shadow you from this point forward."

"Oh wonderful. That's going to make going to the supermarket interesting. I can see the clerk now. 'Excuse me, ma'am. We don't allow jungle cats in here.' And I will say, 'You tell them! I can't.'"

"Yeah, I can see where that might be a little awkward. Or the beauty shop!"

"Oh, dear! What about at the doctor's office? If these cubs think they're protecting me, and the doctor tries to touch me…?"

"Hmmm. I can see where that would be a problem. Let me think on it a bit. We'll have to come up with some kind of a solution."

As if on cue, the cubs both looked at Brandon as if to say, "Don't be in too big a rush to find that solution, Boss."

And so it was. Everywhere Andrea went, even if only a few steps in the house, she had two companions. It reached the point where it was driving her buggy. Finally, she thought of something. She walked out onto the deck, where the cubs followed her. Then quickly, she did a reverse, ducking back inside the house and closed the patio doors behind her. The cubs looked at her as if they had been betrayed, then turned and faced away from the patio doors, but sat in the alert position as if on guard.

"*What in the barbequed hell is going on*?" she wondered.

But she didn't get to wonder about it for very long. Activity at Jungle Cargo was increasing rapidly. Don Houseman was the perfect man to put in charge of construction. With Lorenzo at his side to act as translator, the duo managed to wrangle the best deals on every aspect of construction, beginning with that meandering walkway through the jungle, which at Don's suggestion, had grown to ten feet wide so as to allow for service vehicles to gain access.

Meanwhile, Leticia found the perfect OBGYN for Andrea. Regular appointments were scheduled, and Dr. Sofia Jimeniz made a solid connection with Andrea. The pregnancy was coming along swimmingly. "How do you say in English? 'Without a hitch'," the doctor chided.

Brandon oversaw everything like the benevolent big bwana. No one could remember ever having seen Brandon happier. And while he kept close watch on the entire project, his main focus was on the new house where he and Andrea would live and raise their child.

He kept making "improvements" to the nursery until finally, the nursery became the focal point in the house. Andrea was tempted to say something but knew better. She let her man have his head.

Remarkably, under the critical construction oversight of Don Houseman, the new house was dried in quickly. Several crews worked in concert with one another but were selected according to the category of jobs to make sure they didn't get in each other's way. As soon as the house was dried in, and a roof built, Andrea was posed with the decision of what color(s) to paint the exterior of the structure.

She chose a French Colony blue, with white trim. The paint contractor set about the task with a vengeance to make sure this job was done to perfection. He knew a lot depended on it. Do the house right, he'd get to paint everything else that was being built. Botch the job and he would be on the outside looking in. So, he chose only the best painters to put a brush to the new home of Brandon Shaw and Andrea Granger.

Meanwhile, plumbers were brought in to run pipes in the house. They wouldn't be in the way of the painters.

Electricians and air conditioner contractors followed the plumbers. Then came insulation and sheetrock. Then, trim carpenters, and a real specialty team to help Andrea design the kitchen. Only in this case, the girls, Anna Maria and Suyapa also had a lot of input. After all, they would be essentially running the house and in charge of most of the cooking. They were a little intimidated at first, but soon embraced their challenge with enthusiasm. Also, allowing them to be an integral part of the design made them have a possessive feeling about what was going on, something that had been very rare in their lives.

Aside from the nursery, Brandon's real pride was the

expansive new deck. The deck on the "old" house was reasonably large. But on this new semi "mansion on the beach," the deck was going to be the crowning feature. This, because so much of their lives were spent there, both personal and business-wise. It would be bi-leveled, run out forty feet from the front of the house, and have an entire, covered cook area on the far-right corner. This would include a grill, a pellet smoker, preparation counter and fully functioning sink. There would also be a storage area to keep charcoal, pellets and other cooking implements.

Most of the deck would be covered with brightly colored tarps to help shade against the merciless Central American sun. But the part of the deck that Brandon was the most fussy about was the 'child-proof' deck railing which would be 42" high, feature a wide and highly polished eight inch wide deck railing, and then, the decision was made, in consideration of allowing as much breeze flow as possible, to use four inch mesh galvanized hog wire instead of standard two by two pickets, which would have to be affixed no more than six inches apart. With pickets, breeze would be severely limited.

The hog wire would also be safest for Baby Brandon, or Baby Andrea. This was also the primary consideration when it came to designing the access gate. That, above all, had to be resistant to a child being able to open it.

In many ways, the 'old house' definitely had an influence on this structure. But the new house was much larger, had more rooms, and had improvements on things which had been lessons learned from the 'old house'. For instance, the larder was much bigger here. And there was a lot more cabinet space in this new kitchen.

Within three months, the new house was at the punch-out stage. Final details were completed. Then it was time to have new furniture delivered.

It was precisely at this moment that Andrea arrived home from her doctor's visit, chauffeured by Leticia, with news. She took Brandon aside and said, "Come here, Lover. I have something I want to show you."

Brandon's attention was riveted on the house, but he followed Andrea. "What's going on?"

"Sit!" she said. So, Brandon sank down onto the new sofa in the new living room and eyed his woman.

Andrea withdrew a piece of paper with a laser photo on it which she handed to Brandon. He took the paper, and stared at the image, then he looked up at Andrea, confused. "What am I looking at?"

"Your handiwork, Mr. Shaw," she said with a half-smile.

"My handiwork?"

"Brandon, you're looking at a print-out of a sonogram. That's a picture of our baby."

"It is?"

"Yes, it is." At this point, Andrea sat down next to Brandon. Then she pointed to a small detail on the photograph. "What do you think that is?"

Brandon squinted. "I have no idea."

"Well, Honey, that is his little pecker!"

"What?"

"Brandon, it's a boy."

Brandon looked from the photograph, up, into Andrea's eyes. "A boy?"

"Yes."

"You're sure?"

"Well, according to this sonogram. And I don't think it would lie, even if it could."

Brandon began to breathe heavily. He looked around the room. "A boy! We're gonna have a boy! Un macho! Un baron! Chihuahua! I will have an heir!"

He stood up and walked to the patio doors, slid them

open and walked outside. At the very top of his voice he yelled, "Andrea is giving me a boy!" Then he began to laugh with glee.

Suddenly, he rushed back into the house and took her hands in his. "You know, I was planning a house-warming party. Now we can celebrate two things at once!" He then gently pulled her to her feet, wrapped his muscular arms around her and gave her a tremendous hug.

"With everything I have done to fuck up in this life, I don't know why God decided to smile on me and bring you into my life. But I sure am glad he did."

As soon as she got her breath, Andrea said, "I am too, Honey. I am too."

CHAPTER SIX

Antonio's Brother

IT TOOK THREE DAYS TO ARRANGE THE PARTY. WISELY, Brandon asked for Lorenzo's help in this task. History had shown that Lorenzo was the un-equaled, supreme party planner at Jungle Cargo. This, probably because he took the task to heart. He took extreme pride in his ability to party and be a party planner.

It was a house-warming celebration to be sure. But it was also an announcement that the bun in the oven was a boy, as proclaimed by a huge five foot by twenty-foot-long white vinyl banner with bright blue letters. The banner read: ***A BOY – UN BARON***, so that everyone would be sure to get the message.

A band of Honduran style mariachis played music, and a large pig turned slowly on a spit in the yard. The new, huge deck was dressed out to the max. Guests seem to include just about every person Brandon and Andrea knew. The banker in particular, Sr. Almendarez now viewed the project at Jungle Cargo with particular pride since the Banko Atlantida had now sunk a considerable investment into that project. One could see the pride in his eyes as he looked around at all the construction.

As for the interior of the house, surprisingly, Mary Thompson, previously known as Sad Mary, had demonstrated quite a talent for interior décor and had appointed the new home elegantly, tastefully and within a reasonable budget.

Andrea stood in her new living-room, flanked by the cubs, looking around at her new home. She needed to add her own touches, to be sure. But the house was so beautiful that it took her breath away. She was so happy that she had to hold back tears.

She needed to hug Brandon. She could see him through the patio doors, standing out on the deck chatting with a guest. She decided to join him. He looked around and saw her just as she and the cubs came out onto the deck. She was smiling broadly.

Brandon smiled back and reached for her so he could wrap her in one arm as she joined him and the guest. She didn't need to say anything, yet. She just wanted to hold her man and feel him against her.

It was at that moment that a new figure walked up the steps to the deck. He looked oddly familiar, but Andrea was sure she had never seen him before. Apparently, Brandon was having the same reaction.

The man was tall, about six feet, slender and well dressed, clean shaven. But there was 'something'...

The man paused at the gate to the deck and modestly waved to Brandon. Brandon waved back, then broke away from his guest and Andrea to approach the man and find out who he was.

"Hello," the man said politely as he extended his hand toward Brandon in greeting. "I'm sorry for interrupting your festivities here. My name is Hector. Hector De Alba Munoz. I am the brother of the late Antonio."

Brandon seemed mildly shocked as he reached to accept the outstretched hand of Hector Munoz. "Of course. That's why you look so familiar. Please, let me open this gate for you. Sorry it's a little complicated. We have a child on the way, so even now, all preparations are being made…."

"Of course," Hector said. "Yes, I see the celebration in progress, and that banner. You must have just found out that it's going to be a boy."

"Yeah, we did," Brandon said with a wide smile. Then, "Please, join the party. Can we get you something to drink? Food?"

"Thank you," Hector said. "Yes, I would be most honored to join this gathering and help you celebrate."

"This is a two-in-one fiesta. It's also a house-warming. The paint is barely dry. You can still smell it when you walk inside the house. But please, you need to meet everyone, starting with the hostess of this shindig, and my love, Andrea Granger."

The next several minutes were spent making Hector comfortable, providing him with an ice cold beer and introducing him around, especially to the inner circle; Andrea, Lorenzo and Leticia, Don and Mary Thompson, Doug Bennett and even the girls, Anna Maria and Suyapa.

At one point, Hector asked, "Do you mind if I smoke?"

"Go right ahead," Brandon answered.

Hector withdrew a small, dark cigar from his shirt pocket and lit it. "Just like your brother," Brandon said. "He liked those little cigars."

Hector smiled but said nothing. "I miss him," Brandon said, looking away.

"So do I," Hector said. "We were very close. I understand you were the last person to talk to him."

"I don't know how you know that, but yeah," Brandon affirmed. "He was in a chopper just south of here. He called me on his cell phone. We hadn't talked but a few seconds when all of a sudden, he said there was a duende in the chopper. A couple of seconds after that, the chopper went down. Killed him and the pilot. It was a few hundred yards off the beach at Sambala. I'm the one who dove down and pulled his body out of the chopper."

"I am very grateful to you for that."

Brandon looked at Hector. "He was my friend. I only wish I could have done more." Brandon looked more critically at Hector. "Antonio seldom did anything without a carefully planned-out motive. My guess is, you're the same way. Why are you here? Cuyamel isn't exactly some place you pass en route to somewhere else."

Antonio smiled as he puffed on his small cigar. "No, it isn't. I came here to see you. But we will talk no business today. You are celebrating, and I want to help you do that. That pig-on-a-spit smells delicious. Do you think it's ready? I'm starving!"

Hector De Alba Munoz turned out to be an extremely congenial and likable person. He was also a hungry person and appreciative of good food, complimenting the succulent roast pork multiple times.

Meanwhile, the party was swelling as more people arrived to celebrate the festive occasion, and also to tour the new home. Don Houseman became the unofficial tour guide for visitors, escorting them through the house and pointing out special construction techniques which were designed to make the house resistant to any kind of weather, in addition to making it aesthetically pleasing to the eye.

These were not points overlooked by Hector as he moved slowly through the house, taking in everything Don said about the place. He, like everyone, was duly impressed with the excellent craftsmanship that had gone into the building of Brandon and Andrea's new home.

Lorenzo stayed very close to Leticia throughout the day. It was obvious, Brandon's compound manager was smitten with this woman and both Brandon as well as Andrea predicted an engagement announcement in the very near future.

The former Sad Mary was no longer sad. That part of her life was now far distant in the rear-view mirror, thanks to Andrea's tender heart and intervention. Only she saw through the veil and knew there was still a beautiful heart beating inside the breast of a frustrated, hurting woman, buried in a café in Trujillo. Looking at Mary Thompson today, no one could guess this was the same woman who looked like a hag a few short months ago. Mary walked with pride, was well dressed and stayed close to her man, Don Houseman, who had proven to be the perfect mate for her. They had both been alone and lonely. Thanks to Andrea, that loneliness no longer existed. It was a thing of the past.

CHAPTER SEVEN

We've got to go to Grandpa's House

THE MORNING AFTER THE PARTY, THE VERY FIRST BREAKFAST and meeting was being held forth on the new, expanded sized deck of the new house. All members of the inner circle were dutifully present including the four jaguars; and now, Hector De Alba Munoz, who had been invited to crash in one of the guest bedrooms instead of returning all the way to La Ceiba and being made to endure that nightmare of a road.

A crew of workers had been hired to clean up from the party. They gathered trash from the front yard and beach. A small curl of smoke lazily worked its way upward, remnants of the fire that cooked the delicious pig on the spit. The huge vinyl banner announcing the coming of a son was still strung between two coconut palms, unaffected by the night's moisture.

On the new deck, the girls were giddy as they placed bowls of fresh fruit on long, fold out tables. There were also boiled eggs and other frequent fare. They were excited because this deck was so much larger than the old one and also featured several colorful tarps that offered shade from the sun. This deck was so much more 'fun'!

Hector chose his pieces of fruit carefully and placed them on his plate, which he took to a large square table hosting everyone else in the inner circle.

"This morning 'desayuno'; this is a regular thing with all of you?" Hector asked.

"It is our ritual. Isn't it a wonderful way to start the day?" Don said with a big smile as he salted and peppered a boiled egg.

"I should say so!" Hector agreed.

Lorenzo sat at one side of the table, Leticia at his side. "Oui! Chingow! I should have stuck with beer last night," Lorenzo said.

"I tried to tell you," Leticia chided. "You should have listened."

"I know, I know. I got carried away. All of this stuff that is happening here is starting to overwhelm me. I mean, I never been so pinché excited and happy in my life."

"Just take it in stride," Leticia advised. "Mira! It's like eating a watermelon. You can't gobble the whole thing down all at once. You'd kill yourself trying. Eat the sandia one bite at a time. *One bite a time.* That's how you take it in stride."

"Take it in stride?" Lorenzo looked at Leticia. "Tell me, how am I supposed to take *you* 'in stride', mi corazon? I cannot imagine that."

"Aye, Lorenzo!" Leticia said. "Mira, I have to get out of here and go to work. The Mazapan Hospital awaits!"

With this, Leticia finished off the last bite of her breakfast, kissed Lorenzo, then wished everyone a good day, and left, bouncing down the steps to her car.

"Aye, Chingow," Lorenzo said when Leticia had gone.

"I'm in trouble! I am in love, Jefe. This one is the real thing."

"I can see that," Brandon said with a coy smile. "I would have to agree that you are a very lucky man."

"Yeah," Lorenzo said, looking out at the blue water of the Caribbean. "You know, I never saw myself being in a serious relationship. Maybe some old whore once in a while, but nothing like this. Sabes que… this amazing lady…" He pointed toward Andrea, "she saw something in me that I didn't know was there. And then, she made sure that Leticia and I got together. You know, Doña Andrea, you're a super amazing woman. I am very grateful to you."

Andrea smiled. "You are a good man, Lorenzo. You deserve to have good things happen to you."

Lorenzo raised his coffee cup in the air. "La familia!" he said in a toast.

Everyone at the table, including Hector followed Lorenzo's lead and also raised their coffee cups with the salute, "La familia!"

"I hate to interrupt this fiesta mood," Brandon suddenly said to Hector, "but I can't get it out of my mind that you are here on a mission. Am I wrong?"

"No, you are not wrong," Hector admitted as he bit down on a piece of papaya. "But I think it is something you might want to discuss in a more private setting. Just the five of us."

"Five of us?"

"You, me, Andrea, and those two jaguar body-guards of hers."

"Oh, yeah, okay. Well, why don't we excuse ourselves and go inside this brand new, shining house that my friend Don Houseman built with such amazing talent and dedication."

"Yes, I suppose it is time," Hector said. Then, to the

other people at the table, "No disrespect, my friends. I do hope you will understand and excuse us for a while."

With that, Brandon, Andrea and Hector got up from the table to go inside the house. Sure enough, Andrea was closely followed by the two jaguar cubs.

But an odd thing happened when she passed by Suyapa. The girl whispered in Andrea's ear, "Don Hector is very polite. He made his bed this morning. The room is so clean, it's like no one spent the night there." Andrea looked at the girl, nodded and thanked her in a whisper, then continued on into the house.

In the house, instead of sitting on the sofa, the trio gathered at the kitchen table. Andrea poured fresh coffee for everybody, then took her seat.

"First of all," Hector began. "You are not going to like what I have to say. Neither one of you."

"I had a strange feeling that was going to be the case," Brandon said.

Hector continued. "I am only here because it is absolutely, and I mean *absolutely* necessary. And, what I am about to tell you could possibly affect the future of your son."

"Hold on just a minute," Brandon said. "Future of our son? How did you even know about Andrea's pregnancy, or the fact that it's going to be a son?"

Hector looked straight ahead. "Many secrets are hidden within the darkness of the jungle, Brandon Shaw."

Brandon eyed Hector closely. "I've heard that before."

"Let's keep on track here," Hector said. "The unpleasant truth is you have some unfinished business in The Lost City of The Monkey God."

"What?" Brandon fairly screamed.

"Oh Christ!" Andrea uttered.

"What are you talking about?" Brandon said, startled.

"How could I possibly have any 'unfinished business' there?"

"If you calm down a little, so I can explain, I'll tell you. The bottom line is, you're going to have to go back. And most likely, it would also be best if Andrea came with you. As a matter of fact, it's mandatory."

Brandon was fuming. "You still haven't told me what the fuck you are talking about, Hector?"

Hector waited several moments before resuming. "Brandon, all your life, you've been plagued with, how shall we call it, a bothersome, unwanted connection to an ancient personage at the lost city named, 'Jaguar Man'. You haven't wanted to acknowledge it, even to yourself. But you know what I am talking about. I suspect that Andrea knows too. And that 'connection' is bothering her. It has bothered her since she found out she is pregnant. Well, even before that. It's bothered her since the first day she met you."

At this point, Andrea looked up at Hector, but said nothing. She didn't have to. Her expression said it all. Hector was right. It was written all over her face.

Brandon got up from his chair while muttering profanity, then paced around the room for at least a minute before coming to a stop. "I thought we were through with that fucked up, God forsaken place. I've been there twice now. I can't say that I enjoyed either visit."

"For the sake of your son, you need to go there one more time."

"What the hell does my son have to do with any of this? He isn't even born yet."

"You must face this spirit and make it clear to him that you forsake him. That you disavow any ancient kinship to him. You must forbid him to affect your spirit, or the spirit of your progeny. If you do not do this, the very same curse that has pestered you all your life will be passed on to your son. Do you understand what I am saying? Do you want to risk that? This crazy spirit thinks that you are okay with whatever connection it is."

"How do you know all of this?"

Hector shook his head. "That isn't important. That I do know it is what we have to deal with."

"So, what you're really talking about isn't just a curse, it's a legacy. A bloodline legacy."

"I'm afraid so," Hector said. "We've got to go to Grandpa's house."

"That isn't funny."

"Sorry."

"So, why are *you* here, delivering this message to us? You just showed up out of the blue."

"I like papaya for breakfast," Hector said, smiling. "You were Antonio's friend. You were the last person to speak to him before he died. My brother and I were very close. You were his friend, therefore, you are my friend. Besides, I have a special soft spot for children. I would hate to see yours born with a birthmark, so to speak."

Brandon looked from Hector to Andrea. He stood with his hand propped against the archway frame to the living-room. As he looked at Andrea, he wasn't just looking at her. He was seeking input.

"I think we should go," she said softly, almost inaudibly.

"You do? You think we should go back to that frigging, pile of rocks, lost city in the middle of the goddamn jungle? I'll tell you what this feels like. It feels like I'm sticking my head in the lion's mouth and this just might be the 'one time too many'. Lost City of the fucking Monkey God! Kiss my fuzzy ass! I thought I would never hear about that place again. No! Make that, I *hoped* I would never hear about that place again."

"I don't think we have a choice," Andrea said, not sounding happy.

Brandon looked down at the floor while he thought for several long moments. Finally, "Why does everything have to be so complicated?" He looked up at Hector. "You going with us?"

"Of course. What else?" Hector said. "I think I had certainly better."

"Well, I know one thing. We're not bouncing down that nightmare road in a frapping Jeep. Not with Andrea being in her condition. I'll have to make a call to the La Ceiba airport and wrangle a deal for a chopper."

"That's already been arranged," Hector said softly.

"What?"

"Call it a final gift from Antonio."

"I don't understand."

"You don't need to understand. You just need to get your things together so we can leave at dawn tomorrow morning. If this goes according to Hoyle, we can be back here by tomorrow night."

Andrea suddenly spoke up. "Hold on a second. I have one request. No, make that a requirement. If we're going into the Mosquitia Jungle, I will have to insist that we overnight at the Jungle Inn and visit with Didier. I'd like to tell him the news."

"Not a problem," Hector said with a wry smile. "I have heard wonderful things about this Don Didier. I'm looking forward to meeting him."

"Naja goes," Brandon said.

"Of course," Hector said.

"So do the cubs," Andrea added.

"I have already had an extensive talk with the chopper pilot," Hector said wryly. "I have explained that there isn't a thing to worry about. That he will have three human passengers, and three 'non-human'. It took a few minutes to get him to blink again after I explained what the 'non' human part entailed. But he's alright with it now… I think."

Brandon shook his head. "Anybody besides me see anything a little weird about this excursion we are about to embark upon? We're flying two thirds of the way across Honduras to pick a fight with a green ghost. I must be dreaming. Either that, or out of my mind!"

Everyone laughed, then walked back out onto the deck to deliver the news and make plans for their absence. But as they did, Brandon said softly to Andrea. "How did he know to tell the pilot about the cubs? He hadn't been here yet. There's no way he could have known about the cubs."

"There's no way he could have known about a lot of things," she whispered back.

"So then? What's really going on?"

"Do I really have to tell you?" she said.

"Yeah, yeah, I know. 'Many secrets are hidden within the darkness of the jungle.' Seems like I've heard that one several times now. It's starting to be our theme song."

Lorenzo looked absolutely stunned. "You're going back to that pinché lost city? What in the hell for? You've got enough stuff to do around here for six people. And Andrea is pregnant. It's just too dangerous."

"You're telling me!" Brandon said, with exasperation.

Lorenzo studied the worried expression on his boss's face. "There's something heavy going on that you ain't telling me about. I see it in your face. Do you want to share it with me?"

"No," Brandon said. "I don't think you'd believe me if I told you. I'm not even sure that I do."

"You taking Naja with you?"

"We're taking three of the cats. The only one we're leaving here is Cisco."

"Hijo! You're starting to scare the crap out of me, Jefe. This isn't a trip. It's more like a mission, si?"

"Yeah," Brandon said, as he turned to walk away. "A mission. But a mission to what?"

Intense meetings were held almost non-stop the rest of that day. It seemed as if Brandon was going to be gone a month instead of a couple of days. But admittedly, the timing could have been better. True that the new home was completed, more or less. But now there was the construction of the office to be concerned with. It would be located between the old house and the new house.

This was to say nothing of the three dozen huge flight cages to be designed and built, as well as the attending support/storage buildings close at hand beside each one. There was also a cluster of six small cabins that would be built toward the back of the property. Blueprints had to be firmed up, materials purchased, the list was seemingly endless.

There was also a constant interplay between Don Houseman and the architect draftsmen who were preparing the blueprints. They were thousands of miles away, in the United States, but via use of modern telecommunications, they were practically in the same room. Cell phones and emails and computers used like television phones seemed like a modern-day miracle.

"And here I am going off into the fucking Mosquitia jungle," Brandon said. "The timing just couldn't be worse."

By the time night fell, Brandon was exhausted. Be that as it may, it was almost ritual by now that he and Andrea bathed together, and it was a little more exciting than usual in the very large tiled-in shower in the new house. A large, broad tile bench was perfect for weary bones that needed to relax as the warm water washed over them.

Both Brandon and Andrea were so tired that almost no conversation transpired. But despite the exhaustion and warm relaxing shower, sleep was difficult, especially for Brandon who had trouble sleeping under the best of circumstances. The meetings of that day kept repeating themselves in his head, despite all efforts to close them out.

Then too, there was the worry of what kind of magilla tomorrow would bring. Going back to that infernal Maya archaeological site was the last thing Brandon wanted to do, even if the trip had been for a better reason and didn't involve confronting some ancient spirit. Brandon just had a bad feeling about the place.

CHAPTER EIGHT

Love Is the Strongest Force on Earth

THE CHOPPER SAT DOWN RIGHT ON SCHEDULE JUST PAST dawn the next morning. Everyone started piling on board, including Naja and the cubs, who were reluctant at first. But upon seeing their mother board without hesitation, they hopped right up into the aircraft.

Everyone started strapping themselves in, and then Hector took out one of his black cigars, which he started to light.

Suddenly Andrea spoke up. "You light that thing in here and I will personally shove you out one of those little side windows."

"Sorry," Hector said. "I wasn't thinking."

The chopper lifted off, and they were on their way to the Lost City of The Monkey God.

Ninety minutes later the chopper descended slowly and gently down onto a landing pad at the archaeological site. The jungle seemed inordinately green to Andrea, and lush. This, despite a beehive of activity.

There were twice as many tents set up here as there had been the last time Brandon and Andrea were here. And there were a lot more people, all engaged in one form of archaeological research or another. Some had grids set up with string lines and had crews carefully excavating. Others had tables set up beneath easy-up tents with various objects placed on those tables for research.

As the chopper blades slowly wound down to a stop, everyone began unbuckling their seat belts. All that is except for Brandon. He just sat there, as if in a trance, staring ahead. Finally, after a deep sigh, he unbuckled and started to climb out of the chopper.

"Well, now that we're here, I'm not sure what the hell I'm supposed to do."

"You're supposed to reject the duende," Hector said. "And more than that, you're supposed to make sure he knows that he's rejected. That you want nothing to do with him. You should insult him in some way and tell him to release you from any kinship to him."

"So," Brandon said. "Just hum-drum routine stuff. Insult an ancient relative. I can do that!"

As the Shaw entourage gathered beside the chopper, a man approached them and demanded to know what research team they were associated with. The man was rather rude and brash in his approach. His demeanor caught Brandon the wrong way.

"Just who the fuck are you to come around demanding answers?" Brandon said, as he stared at the man.

"I beg your pardon?" the man said indignantly. "I'm Bernard Simms and I'm the overseer of this entire project."

"Overseer? Well then, go oversee something, and get out of my face."

"See here, you can't just land here because you happen to be some kind of wealthy tourists. This is a restricted area."

Brandon glared at the man. "Tell you what, Bernard,

I'm going to count to three, and if you're still visible by the end of that time, I'm going to have this jaguar here give you a special kind of enema. One… two…"

"You can't do that!" said Bernard Simms, not quite sure of himself.

Brandon never took his eyes off of Bernard Simms, but said to Naja, "Naja, chaan ha!"

When he did, Naja took a couple of steps toward Bernard Simms in an attack posture and emitted a low growl.

Bernard Simms took one look at the golden eyes of Naja, then turned and quickly walked away without another word.

"What did you tell her to do?" Andrea asked.

"To get the asshole's attention," Brandon answered.

"Chaan ha," Andrea repeated. "I'll have to remember that! Chaan ha! Yeah! I like that."

Brandon, now clearly exasperated, said to Andrea and Hector, "Are we ready to get this over with?"

Both nodded yes, and the trio of humans, plus the trio of jaguars, were on their way, walking through the archaeological site in the general direction of the pyramid where Brandon had first, and last encountered the green duende who was apparently the soul of Jaguar Man.

It took close to a half hour to reach the structure which Brandon was relatively sure was the right one. The trio were being followed, albeit at a safe distance, by several people who were obviously researchers and had been alerted by the frightened Mr. Simms.

Brandon paused momentarily before entering through the hole made long ago by archaeologists. Luckily, the same battery powered lighting system that had been placed here months ago was still here. Brandon wondered why that was so for a moment, but no matter. That the lights were here served his purposes now, and lucky for him, since bringing a flashlight had been the farthest thing from his mind.

"Okay, let's get this over with," Brandon said, then he clicked the switch that turned the lights on and ducked slightly to go through the hole in the side of the small building. Once entered, he was followed by Andrea, Hector and three jaguars. Inside, Brandon discovered that time had drained the batteries a great deal, and the light provided was almost one half of what it had been and needed to be. Nevertheless, they moved deeper inside the small structure.

The small group made their way to the rear chamber in the old, musty smelling structure to where the duende was most frequently encountered. Brandon stood there for a moment. Then he asked Hector, "Is there something we can do to wake this thing up and make it 'come forth' or whatever?"

Hector's response was to say, "Báalam máak, Jaguar Man, we call upon you. Appear before us." Hector shook his head. "Sounds kind of hokey, doesn't it?"

"Just a little bit," Brandon agreed. The small group continued to stand there, feeling slightly awkward.

For several minutes there was nothing. Brandon was just about to say, try again. But then there was a strange aura in the room and the duende known as Báalam máak, Jaguar Man began to manifest itself. A nondescript green light and a mist, like a fog glowed for five minutes or more, then began to take shape. Within ten minutes, an Ancient Mayan figure floated before them, looking straight at Brandon, as if waiting for instructions.

His eyes were almond shaped. His forehead was flattened, he wore a royal headdress of quetzal feathers and he was adorned in a jaguar pelt draped over his shoulders and had sea-shell bracelets tied around his legs, just below the knees. In his hands, he held a scepter. He looked angry. This was the moment of truth. Brandon curled his mouth into a scowl and said in his most stern voice, "Okay, you gruesome, green puke sonofabitch! It's time we had a little chat!"

And then, he switched into Pech, the ancient language that he knew how to speak, but never understood how he knew it. The longer he spoke to the duende, the louder his voice became until he was fairly yelling.

Outside of the small structure, a crowd of about a dozen archaeologists and researchers gathered, curious about what was taking place inside, but unwilling to chance any more of Brandon's ire, or a jaguar's wrath, by attempting to go farther.

What they heard was a long diatribe being angrily shouted in a language they did not understand. After a few minutes of this, there was a bright green glow emanating from inside the structure, followed by a rumbling that was so violent, it seemed very much like an earthquake that did not subside quickly.

Following that in the next few moments, Brandon Shaw emerged, followed closely by Andrea, Hector and the three jaguars. The audience stood frozen as the Shaw entourage passed close by them.

"I wouldn't go in there for a while if I were you," Brandon said as he passed by the gawkers.

After Brandon and company had walked fifty feet away, one of the gawkers asked, "How long is 'a while'?"

"Oh, I'd say about fifty years or so," Brandon said without looking back.

Thirty minutes later, they had arrived back at the chopper. Brandon climbed aboard immediately and unceremoniously while muttering to the pilot, "Let's get the fuck out of here as quickly as possible. I hope I never see this God forsaken place again."

"Yes, sir," the chopper pilot replied. Everyone barely had time to get strapped in before the bird lifted off. Brandon, in the passenger seat beside the pilot, leaned over and said, "Do you know where The Jungle Inn is located?"

"Yes, sir. It's about thirty minutes from here."

"Good. That's where we want to go, please," Brandon said loudly, so the pilot could hear him.

The pilot nodded affirmatively, and they were on their way.

Thirty minutes later, the helicopter descended slowly for a feather-lite touchdown in the parking lot of *The Jungle Inn*. A couple of Jeeps and a truck with a tarp covered cargo area, were pulled up in front of the hotel. Brandon assumed these vehicles to somehow be associated with The Lost City but didn't give it another thought.

True to form, Didier stood on the tiled landing of his establishment, ready to greet whoever might be disembarking from the helicopter. But this time, he wasn't sure. Brandon's entrance into the jungle this time had been so sudden that 'the jungle' hadn't had time to inform the man of short stature with such a big heart.

When Brandon climbed out of the helicopter, then turned to assist Andrea as she disembarked, Didier's face lit up like a light bulb.

"Oh, my goodness!" he exclaimed. "Brandon and Andrea!" Then he hollered over his shoulder, "Pedro, get some jungle juice ready! We have some thirsty guests!"

Brandon and Andrea walked quickly across the parking lot and up the stairs to the waiting Didier, who was beside himself. "I can't believe my eyes! It is so wonderful to see you."

He hugged Andrea first, then Brandon. By this time,

the pilot had shut the aircraft down and joined them. Brandon started to make introductions. He said, "Didier, this is our pilot, Jeff. And this other guy is…" He looked around but did not see Hector.

"Is Hector still in the helicopter?" he asked the pilot.

Jeff shook his head no. "I thought he had walked over here with you." Jeff then returned to the chopper and peered through the side window. Seeing nothing, he turned and motioned that no one was left aboard, then walked back to where everyone was standing.

Didier said, "I'll bet he just needed to, well, relieve himself and headed for those trees over there. I've done the same thing from time to time. 'Many' secret spots are hidden within the darkness of the jungle!" Everyone laughed.

"Come on," Didier said. "He'll catch up to us. Right now, jungle juice drinks are ready, and we must celebrate your visit. Oh! I can't believe my good fortune. I'm so happy. I wish I had a full orchestra here to play music for us. But the CD player will have to do. I just got a soundtrack by the Bee Gees."

"The Bee Gees?" Andrea said.

"I know what you're going to say. It's old fashioned. But things wear longer here in the jungle. The tree frogs don't get tired of the same songs as easily as we do!"

More laughter.

Inside the Jungle Inn bar, Didier indicated a large table and Pedro quickly produced a blender full of Jungle Juice specialties, accompanied by snacks. Everyone was served, and Didier asked, "So! What brings you to the Mosquitia Jungle?"

"Well," Brandon said. "That's sort of a long story. We'll get to that. First, Andrea has some news to tell you. Then I and Hector, wherever he is, will fill you in on the other sordid, less pleasant details of this trip."

Didier turned his full attention to Andrea. Looking at him with a smile she couldn't hide, Andrea had the feeling that the very perceptive Didier had already figured it out. Never-the-less she said, "Didier, I'm expecting a child. It's a son."

Didier clasped his short, leprosy damaged hands together and closed his eyes in joy. Tears found their way down his cheeks. "There are no words," he managed to say. Then, as he wiped away tears, he rose and took Andrea's hands in his. "Have you thought of a name yet?"

Andrea looked at Brandon. "Well, no. We haven't gotten that far. There has been a *LOT* going on at Jungle Cargo. Didier, we have got so much news to tell you!"

And so, for the next hour, Brandon and Andrea took turns filling Didier in on the events of the past several months at the compound. This of course included Andrea bragging about her new home and showing Didier dozens of pictures she had taken with her phone.

Didier was particularly impressed with the palm sized phone Andrea carried which also doubled as a camera and miniature computer. "Would this phone reach a satellite?" he asked.

"I think the only thing necessary to make that happen is an antenna attachment," Andrea said. "But I have one of those in my purse. Why don't we try it and find out?"

Andrea reached in her purse and withdrew a special antenna which she screwed onto the phone, then attempted a phone call to Jungle Cargo. Sure enough, there was a clear signal and Lorenzo answered his phone.

"Bueno!" Lorenzo said.

"Lorenzo, this is Andrea."

"Hello, Doña," Lorenzo responded.

"We're at the Jungle Inn. I just wanted to check in and see how things are."

"Everything's alright. All of this construction going on doesn't give me time to... anyway. There was this weird cabron wandering around today. I asked him what he was doing, and he said he was 'looking things over'. Then he said he was Reggie's brother. I don't know who Reggie is. But I told him this is a construction site and to get the hell out of here."

"You did the right thing, Lorenzo. I'll tell Brandon. Listen, Didier wants to say hello to you."

"Didier? Oh man! Put him on."

Andrea put Lorenzo on speaker so everyone could hear. Then she handed the phone to Didier.

"Hola, Lorenzo!" Didier said. "Como manicio?"

"Never better," Lorenzo said. "I'm doing good, Didier, except that Don Brandon is trying to work me to death."

Didier laughed. "It is sooo good to hear your voice, my friend. I'm looking forward to another one of our long talks."

"I'd like that too," Lorenzo said, "But I don't know when that would be. Right now, I'm working twelve hours a day. I sure wish you could see this place."

"Maybe I can before you know it."

The conversation continued for another minute or so, then Didier handed the phone back to Andrea. She said goodbye to Lorenzo and ended the call. Then, she looked at the phone, and at Didier.

"You don't have any kind of communication out of this jungle, do you?"

"Well, we have a computer, which works sometimes, but most of the time not. But no phone."

"Well, you do now," Andrea said. "Didier, this is my gift to you." She handed the phone to Didier. Didier accepted the phone, mouth agape. He handled the instrument like it was a delicate flower. For the next thirty minutes, Andrea went over all the details about what the phone could do and how to make it do them. But as it happened, she just 'happened to have' the instruction booklet with her as well as the charger. If one did not know better, they would have to think that Andrea had this planned.

And of course she did. Didier was one of her favorite people. She admired this little man who was born of leprous parents in the middle of the jungle, suffered the ravages of the disease himself, and yet managed to pull himself up by his own bootstraps, forge a dream and then, miraculously, make that dream come true. On top of it all, he was a true gentleman. A self-made one. And by the word 'true', Andrea meant that there was no pretense about Didier. He always spoke from the heart.

That fondness for this little man is what inspired her to take a side trip here after finding out that a journey into the Mosquitia was inevitable. She couldn't wait to share her news of pregnancy with Didier.

Now, it seemed all of the news had been delivered, but no! There had been so much news about Andrea's condition and all the construction activity at Jungle Cargo that one marvelous thing had been entirely overlooked, odd as it seemed.

"There is one more bit of news to share with you, Didier," Andrea said with a proud smile.

Didier sat, anticipating, looking at Andrea. She indicated the jaguar cubs at their feet. "Meet Naja's cubs. Remember Cisco, whom you named? Well, he and Naja were doing more than just palling around together that day in the jungle."

Didier had been so preoccupied with the sudden, unexpected arrival of his friends and the Santa's sack full of news they brought, that he hadn't given the three jaguars a second thought. Now he looked at them with all the pride of a godfather. He laughed with delight then reached down to stroke their heads and coo for them. And the jaguars seemed to respond to this man with a good soul by rubbing against his legs and looking up at him, then purring as only a jaguar can purr.

After more than an hour, there was still no sign of Hector De Alba Munoz. Didier asked a couple of his employees to take a look around before it got dark and see if they could spot any sign of him. Then, something occurred to Didier.

"Wait a minute! You say this gentleman's name is Hector and he is the brother of Antonio?"

"That's right," Brandon said.

Didier called his men back and cancelled the search.

"What's going on?" Brandon asked.

"Antonio once told me about his brother. They were very close. Then Hector got killed, in the valley of Copan, several years ago. There's a dirt airstrip there, adjacent to the archaeological site and visitors have to walk right across the runway to get to the ruins. Apparently, Hector wasn't watching and walked right out in front of a landing plane."

"You sure he was talking about Hector?" Andrea said.

"Yeah. Hector is the only brother Antonio had."

"Well then, who is this guy?" Jeff, the pilot asked.

"I think he is Hector. Or, *was* Hector," Andrea said.

"What are you talking about?" Jeff said, as Andrea's words began to sink in.

"Let's put it this way; do you believe in ghosts, Jeff?"

"Ghosts?" The full force reality of what had happened sunk into Jeff and the response was not good. The man started to shake wildly and lose control.

"What the hell is going on here?" he demanded. "Are

you people fucking with me? There's no such a thing as ghosts. I'm going to go find that guy right now!"

Jeff got up and started walking toward the front entrance at a fast pace. But before he got there, he slowed down and started to wobble, then stagger, and a moment later, swoon. Jeff fell on the tile floor, out cold.

Two workers in the restaurant, plus Didier rushed to help Jeff. Andrea kept her seat and said, "Doesn't look like Jeff accepted the truth very well."

"I can understand that," Brandon replied. "I'm feeling a little that way myself. I'm just handling it better because this is our second similar experience."

Andrea nodded. "It feels a little like falling off a ladder and never hitting bottom."

"I just hope Ol' Jeff gets a grip before we take off in that bird tomorrow morning."

Didier and his two workers managed to wake Jeff up, then assisted him to a room where he could lie down and recover.

Despite Pilot Jeff's somewhat over the top reaction to apparently interacting with a spirit, Didier managed to arrange for a celebration that evening that would rival anything put on by a four-star hotel in the city. He put everyone that worked for him to different tasks of a feast fit for a king, and this included the three jaguar guests at his hotel whom he took under his wing as if they were his own.

Didier was the perfect gentleman and a perfect host; a miracle considering he had been born of such humble circumstances. He was the son of lepers, part of an outcast colony who had been condemned to the Mosquitia Jungle decades ago.

But sometimes, a person's origin makes no difference. Didier was educated by nuns who had entered the jungle as missionaries. They had brought with them old books and magazines. Magazines that Didier plowed through and read word for word. One of those magazines had an article about hotels. Didier read the article and knew from that moment, he wanted to have his own hotel. He educated himself and then began an impossible quest. He decided he would build a quality hotel right smack-dab in the middle of the jungle. It was his dream, and any sane person would have told him it was impossible. But Didier did not know the meaning of that word. Therefore, against all odds and slowly, piece by piece, he forged his dream into reality.

He did it without consideration of whether or not it would be a financial success. He did it because it was the dream itself that was important. Luckily, as things turned out, there was enough activity going on in the Mosquitia, what with scientists, archaeologists, and an assortment of other people making their way through this labyrinth, that Didier's Jungle Inn became an oasis, a Godsend for weary travelers, regardless of their cause for journey.

But for Didier, that was just icing on the cake. True enough, he wanted visitors to stay at his hotel. The Jungle Inn, however, was proof positive that absolutely nothing is impossible if only one believes in their heart that they can do it.

Now that the hotel was a reality, everything Didier did was done with pride and dignity. Profit was strictly an afterthought, an almost unimaginable concept in today's greed driven society. Absolutely amazing for a little man, disfigured since childhood by the disease passed down from his parents.

Tonight was no exception. The celebration of Andrea's natal announcement was a cause for great happiness at the

Jungle Inn, and Didier was determined to make it a memorable occasion for all. He set the feast with baked oscillated turkey and all the trimmings from the Jungle Inn's own garden. For dessert, there was homemade flan.

As for the jaguars, they each had a tapir leg presented to them, and Didier made sure the large water trough, which he had imported for Naja, was filled with fresh water so the cats could play. It was a night to remember. For music, there was the DVD player with a Beach Boys album, and of course, the Bee Gees.

At one point during the evening, Pilot Jeff managed to appear from his room. "I smelled the good food," he said with a meek smile. Everyone welcomed him to the table. Now that he'd had a chance to rest, good food was just what he needed to get him back on track.

This was as close to a family as Didier would ever get. And it was enough for him. He felt very close to Brandon, Andrea and these jungle cats. Likewise, they felt very close to him. This little man, so scarred from his disease had captured the hearts of his guests.

CHAPTER NINE

Return to A Bird's Nest

By the next morning, Pilot Jeff seemed to be his old self and was ready to fly his passengers back to Cuyamel. The flight was uneventful and went by quickly. The minute the bird sat down on the beach in front of Jungle Cargo, several people were waiting to welcome the return of Brandon, Andrea, the jaguars, and also, they thought, Hector De Alba Munoz.

When they asked where he was, Andrea simply replied, "He decided to stay in the Mosquitia for a while."

The front deck of the new house was now the new meeting place of choice. Thus, installed at a table with coffee and a bowl of pan dulce, Don Houseman asked, "How was your trip? Successful, I hope?"

"I think so," Brandon replied. "At least I hope so. I hope to never see The Lost City of The Monkey God again for as long as I live. How are things shaping up here?"

"Everything is going according to schedule," Don replied. "and in some cases, I think we are a little ahead of projected building schedule. According to Hoyle!"

"Who is this pinché guy, 'Hoyle' that you keep referring to?" Lorenzo asked.

Don smiled. "I'm sorry. There was once a guy named Edmond Hoyle that wrote a book about the rules for playing cards. The phrase caught on. It just means, going by the rules, or things are going according to plan, things are going right."

"Oh, bueno. Now I understand. That's kinda neat. 'Hey, cabron! Things are going according to pinché Hoyle!' Ahoralé!"

Everyone laughed, then Don proceeded to detail the events that transpired during Brandon and Andrea's absence. Construction was indeed progressing well ahead of schedule, and because of Don's extensive knowledge of construction, also slightly under the estimated budget.

As much as Andrea wanted to sit in on the meeting, she was weary, and needed to go take a shower. Leticia arrived as if on cue, so she and Mary Thompson went inside the house with Andrea to assist her with whatever they could, and also no doubt to get knee deep in girl talk.

As the three women closed the patio doors behind them, Don smiled. "You know, Mary has got some hidden talents. She has made a few suggestions regarding construction of the flight cages that makes a lot of sense. Like, a miniature sali-port with two doors, so birds can't escape. Also, she has an eye for landscaping, which is a little premature for the expanded compound, but we are eventually going to need landscaping. By the way, she wants me to talk to you about an idea she has. She thinks the expansion should be called 'THE BIRD'S NEST'. Kind of interesting, don't you think?"

"I like it," Brandon said with a smile. "Everything around here should have a name. It's better than just saying, 'at the main house', or, 'in the compound'."

Don's smile changed to something more, something deeper. "You know, I am eternally grateful to Andrea for bringing Mary into my life. I'll tell you truthfully, Brandon, I'm in love with her. That's something I never thought would happen again after my wife died. I didn't think it was possible.

"Especially at my age. I mean, just look at me. I'm no spring chicken. Time really kicks the dog shit out of you. I was looking at an old picture of myself the other day and thought, gawd-o-mity, where is that guy? What's happened to me? I was good looking when I was thirty. But thirty ain't happening no more. That train left the station. It's funny though. No matter what the outside of this old bod looks like, the human heart is indominable. And I've found love again. It's a blessed miracle."

"I'm happy for you, Don. You've been good for her too. You never saw that woman as Andrea and I did, hidden away in that living tomb of a café she owned in Trujillo. She doesn't look like the same person anymore. That's partly due to my little old miracle worker, Andrea, and in part, due to you. She saw you and her heart started to beat again. I've never seen anything like it."

Don laughed a small laugh. "Brandon, I'm going to ask her to marry me."

"What?"

"Yep! I've decided. Oh, I know it's not necessary. Not at our age, well especially my age. But I want her name to be the same as mine. I want Mary Thompson to be Mary Houseman."

Brandon grabbed Don by the shoulders "Don, that's fantastic! Oh my God! You have just made my day. Who else knows?"

"No one," Don said. "Just the people sitting at this table. Me, you, Lorenzo."

"I want to arrange the wedding reception," Lorenzo said with excitement and pride. "Chinelas! You talk about blowing the lid off the mother fucker! This is gonna be a fiesta like you ain't never seen in your pinché life." Then he laughed and yelled, "Ahooooah!"

Both Brandon and Don laughed so loud that it alerted the women. Leticia opened the patio door and stuck her head out. "Que paso aqui?" she asked.

"Oh, nothing in particular," Lorenzo lied. "We just having men talk and telling chistés."

"Aye, hombres!" Leticia said, then went back inside and closed the patio doors.

"When you gonna ask her?" Lorenzo asked in a low voice, being careful.

"Tonight, with your help," Don said to Lorenzo.

"Sure. What can I do?"

"I want to have a romantic dinner, but I don't want to go into town on that nightmare of a road to do it. Brandon, I was kind of hoping maybe we could have a patio dinner here on the deck. Lorenzo, if you could get hold of some of your musician buddies, a trio. We could use Brandon and Andrea's safe return as a decoy. Also, get a couple of those guys passing by the house in cayucos to sell us some of their lobsters. I see the seven of us dining here on the deck, because of course, Doug must come also."

"Oh, my Lord, yes!" Brandon said. "Lobster, wine, music. But somehow, we have to get the girls in on it because we're going to need their help."

"Yes," Don agreed. All three men got their heads together to plot the perfect evening, a set up to be sure. Staging a moment for this friend who had become a de facto member of the jungle Cargo family.

Fate played perfectly into the hands of the three men. Sure enough, a lobster fisherman passed the front of the house in his cayuco right on time. The hull of his carved-out canoe was fairly filled with large, three to five pounder spiny lobsters. Don bought them all. For this dinner/celebration, he wanted to make sure everyone ate and ate well.

Lorenzo summoned the girls, Anna Maria and Suyapa, out onto the deck and shut the patio doors behind them. This was presumably to instruct them about a major deck clean-up, and in fact, that was part of it. But Lorenzo also filled them in on the plot and instructed them about what was needed for the evening. They couldn't suppress their delight, albeit Lorenzo cautioned them to take care not to spill the beans. They were always giggling about one thing or another, so Lorenzo didn't see this as too much of a problem.

By evening, predictably, Lorenzo had managed to secure all the arrangements including the trio of musicians to serenade the venue of love.

Don and Mary arrived on time. They had gone to their house to shower and clean up. Mary had been told this small celebration was a welcome home for the travelers, and she bought it. She dressed very tastefully in a pink sun dress and looked very pretty for the evening's festivities. Don wore blue shorts and an off white guayavera shirt.

By now, Brandon had managed to corner Andrea, well out of earshot of Mary, and fill her in. After that, he corralled Doug Bennett. Lorenzo had done the same with Leticia. Everybody knew exactly what was going on, except Mary.

The seven people were gathered around the large square table on the deck. The fourth side had been left open to make serving easy. Dinner went perfect, according to plan. The lobster was brought out, cooked to perfection, grilled over an open pit fire. The atmosphere was very up-beat, happy. A lot of laughter went back and forth.

Side dishes included fried platanos, and a green salad with home-made salad dressing from Brandon's own special recipe which he called, 'Maxim's green magic'.

The wine was a white chardonnay, served chilled in a champagne bucket.

Dinner was relaxed and filled with friendly chatter about a myriad of subjects. Finally, without knowing it, Mary hit the trigger.

"This is so nice," she commented. "And what a special treat having this trio here, serenading everyone. It just feels like so much. But I guess part of it is to celebrate your pregnancy, Andrea."

"No, that's not it," Don interjected.

"What?" Mary said, turning her head to look at Don and see what he was talking about.

"I said, Andrea's pregnancy is not the reason for the musicians. Not this time. We've already done that."

"Oh, I'm sorry. Well then, what is the reason?" Mary asked, holding her wine glass in one hand.

"This is!" Don said, then he reached in his pocket and withdrew a small box containing a ring. He got down on one knee. "Mary," he began. "the biggest surprise of my life happened when I met you. I had no idea that I could ever love again. But I love you. You are my today, and my tomorrow. You are the keeper of my dreams, and I want you to be my wife. Will you marry me?"

Mary was stunned. This was the last thing in the world she was expecting. She looked around the table at everyone's expressions to see if this was real. Everyone, including the musicians had fallen silent, waiting for her response. Then she looked back at Don.

"I must be dreaming," she said, almost in a whisper. "I

never thought… Oh my God! Yes, of course I'll marry you. Yes, yes, yes!"

And with that, Don opened the small box he was holding in his hand, withdrew a beautiful gold ring with a pear-shaped diamond, and slipped it on Mary Thompson's finger. With that, the trio began singing a happy song, and everyone at the table cheered. So did the girls, who had been standing close by.

Mary looked as if she were in shock. She turned to Andrea and began to cry. "A year ago, my life was at its end. I was miserable. Lord, *beyond* miserable! I lived day to day and didn't even know the reason for it. Then you came into my life. You, with your good heart and keen intuition. I don't know how to ever thank you. There are no words. And even if there were, they would not be enough."

"Seeing you happy is all the thanks I need," Andrea said as she held Mary. "That's all the reward I will ever need."

"Hijo!" Lorenzo said. "I've never seen anybody actually propose to a woman before. That was beautiful. I mean, pinché beautiful. Don, you are a real gentleman."

"Well, thank you, Lorenzo," Don said. "Right now, I feel like my whole body is electrified. I feel young again. And like Mary, I am eternally grateful to Brandon and Andrea for just accepting me and taking me into their lives without hesitation. In a way, it feels like I have come home. I can't ever remember being this happy." He looked at Mary with love in his eyes, and she returned his gaze with equal love.

"Pushilé!" Lorenzo said with envy. "I want what you two have!"

"Well then, why don't you ask me to marry you?" Leticia said, as she hit Lorenzo on the shoulder.

Lorenzo looked at his girlfriend and his eyes grew wider. "Would you say yes?" he asked.

"Why don't you ask me and find out," she challenged.

"I'm not sure this would be an appropriate time," Lorenzo said. "This is Don & Mary's night. I don't want to distract, I mean, I don't want to steal their thunder."

"You wouldn't be stealing our thunder," Don said. "We've got our thunder. You can't un-ring a bell!"

Laughter.

Lorenzo looked at everyone else at the table, seeking an answer. Or perhaps seeking approval. Everyone at the table plus the girls, the trio and the jaguars, who had been witness to this exchange, had fallen silent for the second time, waiting for Lorenzo to do something.

"I'm not prepared," Lorenzo said. "I don't have a ring to give you."

"Oh, my gosh!" Leticia said. "Mira, do you have love to give me?"

"I love you more than the morning sun and the smell of orchids," Lorenzo answered.

"Ooohhhh, how romantic!" Leticia said with a broad smile. "I didn't know you had it in you! Entonces? Ask the question, silly boy. 'If' I say yes, then you can get the ring tomorrow. I'll help you!"

Lorenzo took a deep breath, looked up as if asking help from above. "Alright…Bueno, Leticia, will you please marry me?"

"If that sun you talked about rises tomorrow, I will marry you," Leticia said with a huge smile.

Lorenzo was in shock. He turned his head slowly toward the other guests at the table and said softly, "Hijolé! I wasn't planning for this to happen. I'm engaged to be married! Me. Lorenzo. I'm going to have a wife. I'm going to be a husband."

"Yes, and with any luck, a father," Leticia said authoritatively, but with a smile.

Lorenzo's eyes grew even bigger as he began to smile. Everyone at the table laughed.

"Well now," Don said to Brandon. "You're the only one left."

Brandon was sipping his beer. "What do you mean, 'the only one left'?" he asked.

"I mean… Doug, sitting over there so quietly, observing all of this, is already married. Of *ALL* the people sitting at this table tonight, you're the one with the most reason to get hitched. After all, you have a son on the way. A progeny, an heir. Don't you want that heir to have your name?"

Brandon looked at Andrea sitting next to him. "Of course I do! I have to admit, it's been on my mind. What do you think?" Brandon looked imploringly at Andrea.

"What do you mean, asking me, what do I think? I'm in a family way. Or, as Mary likes to put it, I'm 'knocked up'. So, yeah, we've gone this far. I'd kind of like to be able to call my family in Indiana and tell them the good news, and that the child is not… without a name."

"Then you mean you'd marry me if I asked you?"

"Well, now, I just don't know, Brandon Shaw. I'm going to use Leticia's line. Why don't you ask me and find out?"

"What about a ring?"

"Details, details."

"Alright… Andrea Granger, will you marry me? Will you take my name? Will you be my wife?"

"Hmmm. Let me think about it. Uh, yeah! Yes, I will marry you. I will be your wife."

"Well that's real good," Brandon said as he reached into his pocket and withdrew a small jewelry box, opened it and withdrew a gorgeous gold band with a large diamond. "Because otherwise, I wouldn't know what to do with this!"

Then he gently took Andrea's left hand and slipped the ring on her finger.

"What the hey?" she said. "Was this a set up?"

Brandon grinned. "Well, when Don told me of his plans today, it got me to thinking. But actually, I've been carrying this ring around since our trip to Atlanta."

"What?"

"The truth is, I wanted to marry you, even before you told me you were knock—in a family way. I've just been trying to find the right moment. What do you think inspired all this change in direction for Jungle Cargo?"

"You mean?"

"Yeah, I mean!"

"Oh Brandon!" Andrea put her arms around Brandon's neck and pulled him to her, squeezing him tight.

CHAPTER TEN

The Plan Makers

While the men of Jungle Cargo worked feverishly on construction of the new facility, the three women, Andrea, Mary and Leticia worked equally as hard on plans for a triple wedding. And there was excitement overload as the planning made headway.

In one way it was going to be three events in one. Don was Jewish, Lorenzo and Leticia were catholic, while Andrea was Protestant. Brandon didn't care. He believed strongly in God but had never really affiliated himself with a church.

It was decided that the triad wedding would take place on the beach in front of the new house. Three connecting wedding arches would be constructed, and each respective arch would be festooned with the bride's favorite flower. For instance, Mary loved gardenias. Leticia's favorite flower was roses, and Andrea's favorite was orchids.

The three women gave equal attention of detail to every aspect of the ceremony. There would be three wedding cakes. The women flew to Tegusigalpa together to look for just the right wedding dresses. If observers didn't know better, they would have thought these tireless three were planning to overthrow a government.

As it turned out, finding a Rabbi in Honduras presented a problem. After all, it is a Catholic country. So, arrangements were made to fly a Rabbi in from Miami, where there is no shortage of Rabbis.

Details! There was no shortage of them and as it turned out, the three brides to be were excellent at details, never overlooking even the smallest one and making copious notes as they went so that nothing would be forgotten or overlooked.

The women had taken over the dining room table in the new house, forcing the men to move their blueprints and other papers onto two large folding tables that had been shoved together and made to stay connected with duct tape.

"We realllly need an office!" Brandon said, a little exasperated.

"Wouldn't matter," Don said. "They'd take that over too."

"Yeah, I guess you're right," Brandon said as he watched the three ladies in conference at the dining-room table. "They don't even know we're here."

Don smiled. "I hope we're invited to the wedding!"

Just at that moment, there was the sound of a truck horn tooting. It was a delivery driver with a load of lumber from Fereteria Atlantida, the lumber yard in La Ceiba. He had pulled up in front of the new house, unsure of where to offload the building materials.

But when Don went downstairs to talk to him, a frown developed as he looked at the materials the driver had brought.

"What the hell?" he said, angrily. "Are you people looking for a place to dump your trash? These materials aren't worth a shit. Look at those warped boards, and really bad barky corners. This is a pile of scrap. Take it back to the lumber yard."

"But I have instructions!" the driver protested.

"I don't give a damn what your 'instructions' are. I'm giving you *new* instructions," Don said. "There is no way you are going to unload that pile of junk lumber on this property. Now get out of here. What's the owner's name of that lumber yard?"

"Don Ezekiel," came the frustrated reply, as the driver got back in his truck.

"Ezekiel," Don muttered as he walked back up the steps. "Well, me and Ezekiel are fixing to have a donkey barbeque. Try to pawn off that crap on Jungle Cargo? Bullshit!"

When Don was back upstairs, he grabbed his phone and looked up the listing for Fereteria Atlantida, pressed the button and waited. When they answered, he asked for Ezekiel, but was told the man had left for the day. Don would have to try again the following morning.

Everybody called a recess to their respective work on Friday afternoon and went their own way. Brandon and Andrea wound up on the deck with the jaguars, sipping a cocktail, while resting in chaise lounges. Well, that is, Brandon was sipping a cocktail with alcohol. Andrea was sipping a cocktail made of guayavera nectar. No booze! She was determined this was going to be a healthy child. No booze, no caffeine, watching her diet, all embraced by the proud mother-to-be, and with careful guidance by Leticia.

Small talk was the order of the day. Then something caught Brandon's eye. He started watching a frigate bird that was floating stationary on in-shore air currents about a hundred feet above them.

"Seems like there are always frigate birds hovering right above this place," he observed.

Andrea looked up, shading her eyes with her hand. "Yes, there are. I've noticed them too."

"That gives me an idea," Brandon said. "I think I am going to name this house, Frigate Point! What do you think?"

Andrea nodded approval. "I like it. Except that you might want to modify it to 'Frigate Bird Point'."

"Why's that?" Brandon asked.

"Well, Frigate Point might be misunderstood as a slight play on words."

"Ohhh!" Brandon said as the alternate meaning sunk in. "Yeah, you're right. So, then, Frigate Bird Point it is. I'll get a wooden placard made to nail onto the front deck railing."

"Let's toast it. Frigate Bird Point," Andrea proposed.

"Frigate Bird Point!" Brandon said, and clinked glasses with her. He took a sip of his drink and then asked, "So, where are you gals on the wedding plans?"

"I'd say we've got about two thirds of it done," Andrea said. "It's been a lot of work, but then, it's been a labor of love."

"It's been interesting to watch," Brandon said with a smile. "I've never seen three women work so hard on a project and tempers not boil over even once."

"Oh no. It's drawn us closer together. We're like three sisters now. Anyway. No planning tomorrow. I've got to go to town. Doctor's visit."

"It's Saturday."

"I know. Leticia has it all arranged. She's been a great help with all of this."

Brandon's mood suddenly changed slightly. His expression changed to one of concern. "It's almost too perfect."

"What is? What do you mean?"

"I mean this. I've never seen anything around this place go this smoothly, this flawlessly; the construction is sailing along, thanks to Don, like it had been rehearsed a dozen times. That scene the other night right here on this deck where not one, but three… count them, *three* couples became engaged. Mine and Don's was planned. But Lorenzo's engagement came out of left field. Wham! It was just too wonderful. I feel very much like we have an extended family, and I love it. It's a damn good feeling. Maybe my apprehension is just fear that the bubble will pop. I don't know. Too much has happened in my past. Gotta forget about that. Things are different now."

"Well, good things come back to people who do good things. This new preserve you're building is wonderful, Brandon. I've never really said this to you, but I'm very proud of you. What you're doing is a very good thing. I don't know if you've changed, or if it's just that the old rusty Brandon is being set aside and the one who has always wanted to do good things is being allowed to emerge, to grow. Whatever, it's amazing to watch. I'll be right by your side all the way as your wife, your partner, your best friend and closest confidant."

Brandon watched Andrea as she talked to him and stroked his hair. He felt deep emotions of love that he never knew he had.

"You rescued me," he said reverently. "You could have slam dunked my ass right into hell. But you didn't do that. Sometimes I ask myself why."

"Because I saw goodness in you. I believed if I changed the circumstances, that good person would emerge, and that's exactly what happened. I am vindicated. Well, actually, I am vindicated, engaged to be married and pregnant!"

"You left something out."

"What?"

"You're also unbelievably amazing. Everywhere you go, you do good. It's just a natural part of you, like sunshine brings warmth and makes the flowers grow."

Andrea smiled, but said nothing as she looked into Brandon's eyes, then pulled him to her for a long, deep kiss.

CHAPTER ELEVEN

The Premonition

SATURDAY MORNING, ANDREA WAS UP EARLY. SHE WAS ravenously hungry and wanted breakfast. By now, coffee was off her list, so she asked Suyapa to make her a liquado, known in the states as a 'smoothie'. Suyapa set about cutting fresh mango, papaya and banana, and placing it into the blender along with ice and a little cold water. She turned the blender on and moments later, Viola! A beautiful, tasty, yet healthy, liquado.

This and fresh pan dulce seemed to satisfy Andrea's hunger. She sat at the big square table on the deck. Brandon joined her, coffee cup in hand, Naja ever present. So were the cubs, still flanking Andrea. Brandon kissed her, then sat in the chair next to her. It wasn't long before Lorenzo showed up with Cisco at his side, then Don and Mary. Don brought a bowl of his famous deviled eggs. They were well received all around the table.

Doug also showed up but made the announcement as he ate that he needed to fly back to Florida for a while. There were too many problems piling up in his absence. He would be leaving right after breakfast but made a solemn promise that he would be back in time for the triple wedding, and even bring Francis, his wife.

After breakfast and a pleasant chat with everyone at the table, then telling Doug goodbye and wishing him a safe flight, Andrea excused herself and went inside to make preparations for her trip into La Ceiba. She re-emerged from the house a half hour later, her purse strap over her shoulder and fresh makeup applied. Saying goodbyes to everyone, she then bent down to kiss Brandon. When she did, Brandon went pale, grabbed the arms of his chair and sat forward.

"What's the matter?" Andrea said.

"I dunno," Brandon answered. "Something…it was like a dark shadow. A premonition. Andrea, I want you to stay here. Don't go into town right now."

"Brandon! I don't have any choice, Honey," she said. "I have an appointment. This is important. You're just reacting to everything that's been going on around here. Besides, I'm a big girl. Remember?"

With that, she kissed him again and went skipping down the steps to the Jeep. Brandon still felt apprehensive, even when he heard the Jeep's motor start up and Andrea drive away.

"Something's wrong," he said to no one in particular. "I just feel it."

Brandon didn't have long to dwell on his ill-rest. Workers began to arrive, and a brief meeting was held on the deck as Don Houseman gave instructions about what the focal point of the day was to be. Work began very quickly, as little instruction was required at this point. The work needed was a continuation of where the crew had left off the previous day.

Then, Don made a phone call to the owner of the lumber yard in La Ceiba and had a come-to-Jesus discussion with him about the material that was brought to Jungle Cargo the previous day.

"I would be willing to bet that at this moment we are one of your biggest Dollar volume customers. That is, Limpira. So, we deserve better service."

"What do you mean Señor Houseman?" Don Ezekiel sounded alarmed.

"What I mean is, if you treat me like I just got off the bus one more time, I'm going to stop buying lumber from you and go to your competitor. You brought me a truck load of crap yesterday. Grade 'C' stuff with warped boards that looked like you'd had them lying around in the yard for six months. There were barky corners. Some of the boards didn't have corners at all. *Don't play dumb.* You know exactly what I'm talking about because I wouldn't let your driver unload. I sent him back with the entire load.

"Look, here's the way it is; I've got too much to do. I need to be able to depend on my suppliers. If I can't trust you to give us the quality we're paying for, I have no choice except to get somebody that I don't have to nursemaid. Now what's it going to be?"

"I certainly don't want to lose your business. I will look into this the minute we hang up and from now on, I will personally inspect each load of materials before it leaves this property."

"Alright, we'll see. Now, I still need that stuff that I ordered yesterday. How fast do you think you can get it out here?"

"I'm on it even before we hang up the phone," Don Ezekiel said. "We'll be loaded and on the way within the hour. You have my word. In fact, I'll personally bring it to you so that I can apologize to you in person."

With that, the call ended. Brandon had overheard Don dress down the lumber yard owner and smiled. He considered himself very lucky indeed to have this seasoned professional working with him. It was also nothing short of a miracle to have someone on his side who was not driven by a profit motive, someone who took this project as personally as he did.

An hour and a half later, a lumber truck with the sign *FERETERIA ATLANTIDA* painted on the door pulled through the gate of Jungle Cargo, driven by the same driver who had been there the previous day. But this time, the owner of the lumber yard was in the passenger seat, looking apprehensive.

As soon as the truck rolled to a stop, the owner climbed down, a clipboard in one hand, looking for Don Houseman. Don appeared from the building site and looked at the load of materials. This time, there was a world of difference. This lumber had obviously been hand selected. Don had a brief discussion with the lumber yard owner and then told him where he needed the materials offloaded. The driver quickly went to the spot indicated and began the unloading process. After unstrapping the lumber, the driver pulled a lever on the side of the truck and the bed began to tilt.

By now, Brandon had joined Don and the lumber yard owner. Don Ezekiel was making profound apologies and swearing an oath that yesterday's mistake would never, never be repeated.

"I'll tell you something else," Don Ezekiel said. "Heads are going to roll over this. Not only you, but no customer should ever have the quality of lumber, like yesterday, delivered to them. Every bit of that was cull stuff that is supposed to be burned. I don't know how it wound up on a delivery truck going anywhere, except to the junk yard. Our company is honorable, Señor. We have a reputation and I intend to get to the bottom of this. There is definitely larceny involved here somehow."

It was clear that Don Ezekiel was sincere. He was rightfully concerned that some kind of debauchery was going on behind his back in the yard, and his company was paying the price in more ways than one.

As Don Ezekiel was walking away, toward his truck, he said, "I see that one of your vehicles must have motor problems. If you would like, we have a winch here on this truck. We could pull the Jeep up onto the bed of the truck and haul it into town for you."

Brandon went cold. "One of our vehicles?"

"Yes, I think it is yours."

"A blue Jeep?"

"Yes, a blue Jeep?"

"Where is it?" Brandon demanded.

"On the main road, about four or five kilometers after you turn toward La Ceiba."

Lorenzo's truck was the closest vehicle, sitting in the driveway next to where the Jeep normally parked, but Brandon didn't have a key. Brandon yelled at the top of his voice, "*Lorenzo!*"

Lorenzo came walking toward them from the building site where he had been overseeing workers. "Si, Jefe?"

"Come quick," Brandon said. "We may have a problem."

"Problem? What kind of problem?"

"I don't know, yet. But you've got to take Don and me up to the main road, toward town. Hurry!"

Moments later, Lorenzo's truck left Jungle Cargo in a cloud of dust. Brandon explained what Don Ezekiel had said to him.

"Oh shit!" Lorenzo said. "I just knew things were going too smooth around here."

Within a few minutes, Lorenzo came skidding to a stop behind the blue Jeep. By now, some curious Indians were milling around, looking the Jeep over. The vehicle was pointed West, toward La Ceiba, but not really pulled over on the side of the road as if the stop had been intentional or voluntary. Andrea was gone, but one of her sandals was being held in an Indian's right hand.

Brandon snatched the sandal and demanded, "Where did you find this?"

The Indian indicated by pointing to a spot on the ground next to the driver's side. Brandon glared at the Indian, then looked inside the Jeep. Andrea's purse was also missing.

"The cops!" Lorenzo said.

Brandon agreed as he pulled his cell phone from his belt saddle. "Yeah, this time we need the cops!" Brandon pressed the button for emergency assistance. A minute later, the police were en route. Meanwhile, Lorenzo shooed the Indians away, advising them they wouldn't want to be there when the fuzz showed up because they would be made to answer too many questions.

Meanwhile, Don got on his phone and called Mary to advise her of what had been found and also to warn her to be on the alert for trouble. She needed a body-guard. All of the women at the compound did. But the only person present was the new kid, Adan. He was skinny and barely five feet tall. He hardly qualified to guard anybody despite the ever-present machete in his hand.

A quick discussion of the problem between the three men resulted in Lorenzo making a phone call to a friend of his in Sambala who was one of the biggest black men anyone had ever seen on this part of the coast. Lorenzo instructed him to go to Jungle Cargo with a few of his friends and "Protect all of the women there like they were a sacred treasure."

Don then called Mary a second time to let her know guards were on the way, and to not panic when a giant black guy named Esteban Morales showed up.

At that point, the first of several police vehicles arrived on the scene. Brandon began to tell the Lieutenant about the morning's events and show him the Jeep. Police immediately roped off the area around the Jeep with a yellow crime scene tape, then prohibited anyone, even Brandon and party from entering the area. Crime scene investigators arrived and began a meticulous gathering of anything that might be useful as trace evidence.

They covered the Jeep inside and out with a fine blue dust that was used to expose fingerprints. At some point, the Lieutenant informed Brandon, Doug and Lorenzo that they would all have to be fingerprinted for purposes of elimination.

It was at this point that a helicopter began to hover overhead, seemingly looking for a place to land. Brandon shaded his eyes, looked up and recognized the U.S. government seal under the nose of the chopper.

Moments later, the chopper picked a place directly in the middle of the dirt road as a landing site. It was no great surprise when a very serious looking David Harkness climbed out of the machine, wearing a beige suit. He came walking toward Brandon at a quick stride.

When he approached, he didn't bother with cordialities. He looked straight at Brandon and said, "Fill me in on what happened here."

Likewise, Brandon cut straight to the chase and began giving David a detailed account. That is, until the Lieutenant walked up to them and demanded to know who David was.

"And just who are you, Señor?" said the lieutenant with a very indignant look on his face.

As he pulled his ID and badge from his suit breast pocket, he said without bothering to look at the Lieutenant, "David Harkness, DEA. The woman who is missing used to be a DEA agent. Therefore, she is under the protection of the U.S. Government in perpetuity. I have a crew en route to conduct our own investigation. We will be glad to work in concert with you and share information, providing you work with us also."

"This is Honduras," the Lieutenant said. "You have no jurisdiction here."

That's when David Harkness looked straight at the lieutenant. "I don't give a fuck if this is your grandmother's back yard. An ex DEA agent is missing, and we *will* investigate. You got that? Or would you prefer a phone call from Tegusigalpa. We can do it either way. But either way, I don't have any more time to fuck around. Now, what have you got so far?"

The Lieutenant from La Ceiba stood stock silent for a minute, then made the wise decision to not buck this gringo in the beige suit. The man looked far too serious to mess with. The Lieutenant opened up and began to detail what steps had been taken so far.

David listened for a minute. Just then, a second helicopter arrived and landed behind the first one. The road was completely blocked. Someone from the La Ceiba police department made the decision to tear down the barbed wire fence running beside the road and create a makeshift detour around the site.

It didn't take long before a reporter showed up from the local La Prensa and started taking pictures. David pointed at one of his men, then pointed at the reporter. David's agent approached the reporter, seized his camera and had a short, but very meaningful discussion with him. The agent also removed the memory chip from the reporter's camera and confiscated it as evidence. Looking very put-out, the reporter quickly climbed back in his car, turned it around and headed back to La Ceiba.

Then David turned back to Brandon. "Do you have any idea who might have done this?"

"Yes, I do," Brandon said. "When Andrea and I were in Atlanta a few months ago, this weird sonofabitch showed up saying he was the brother of that voodoo priest who used to operate out of Sambala. He said his brother was missing and started asking me questions about it as if I might know something."

"Why would he think that?"

"Because I am the one who shamed him. He used to call himself 'Smoke Jaguar', a name he borrowed from an ancient Mayan ruler of Copan. Anyway, I whipped his ass right there in front of the villagers of Sambala. I took away his 'mojo'. It instantly exposed him as a phony and put him out of business. So, this bird shows up who says he is Smoke Jaguar's brother. Wants to know if I have any information about his whereabouts. After that, the brother, Oswald Carlson, I think he said his name was, showed up here in Honduras. I had a confrontation with him that didn't end well for him."

"What do you mean?"

"Ah...well, as he was leaving, Naja snuck up behind him. I stopped her in time, but she roared like thunder *right* behind him. It scared the shit out of him. I'm afraid that isn't a euphemism. Since then, he's been spotted a few times, just standing around, watching the house from the beach. He obviously thinks he has some bone to pick. Maybe lunacy runs in his family."

"Where was this so called temple?"

"In Sambala.

"Let's go," David said. "I want you to show me where."

"What? In that helicopter?"

"No. We'll go in your truck. These guys will be here at least another hour. Then we're going to load the Jeep up and take it to a warehouse in La Ceiba that we're using for a lab. You can have it back in a couple of days, when we get through with it."

David gave brief instructions to a second-in-command, then the four men piled into Lorenzo's truck and headed for Sambala.

When they pulled up in front of the now defunct "Temple of The Black Jaguar," and disembarked the truck, it was no surprise when they saw that the old blue building appeared uninhabited. One of the front double doors was ajar. No big surprise. There were only round holes in the doors where doorknobs were supposed to be.

"So, this is the place?" David said.

"Yeah, this is it," Brandon replied, as he looked disdainfully at the abandoned building.

There was a trucha (a Central American version of a general store) located directly across the dirt street from the old 'temple'. That is where David Harkness went first. He walked in the front door, immediately spotted the owner leaning on the counter, watching all the action in the street and asked him, "Have you seen any people going in or out of that building across the street lately?"

"A few weeks ago," the store owner answered, "but not lately. People around here are afraid of that place."

"Really. What are they afraid of?"

"You know. Used to be some kind of a voodoo place. A really strange chingo did all kinds of weird stuff, chanting, had a cage with Don Brandon's black jaguar." The store owner pointed at Brandon. "He would beat on the cage to make the jaguar roar and scare the shit out of people. Then he'd tell them that if they didn't give him Limpiras, the jaguar would visit them in their dreams."

"Why didn't somebody try to stop him?"

"Everybody afraid of him, even the policia. Then one day, Don Brandon come and knock him clear off that cement porch. Don Brandon not afraid of nothing."

"So, who was the last person you saw go in that building?"

"Another weird chingo that look like the voodoo guy. He go in and out the place for a few days, then he don't come back no more. At least two, maybe three weeks since I seen him."

"Have any locals gone in there since?"

"Hell no. Like I say, people around here scared of that place."

"Great. Thanks for your help. Listen, there are fixing to be a lot of men come here. Don't let it worry you. They'll do their jobs and be gone before sundown. However, here's my business card. If you ever see that weird guy come here again, please call me right away."

The store owner nodded his head that he understood and accepted the business card. David walked out. Once he rejoined Brandon and the others, he pulled a special walkie talkie from his pocket. He issued instructions to someone, and a few minutes later, the helicopter hovered overhead, looking for a place to land. Also, several vehicles came racing into the area, all coming to a stop in a cloud of dust behind Lorenzo's truck.

Within minutes, the old blue building had been cordoned off with bright yellow crime scene tape. Dozens of men, some in suits, others in street clothes, but with vests that read *DEA* on the back, swarmed the building, performing meticulous investigative tasks. The structure was dusted for fingerprints inside and out, all footprints photographed, and other swab samples taken, presumably for DNA testing.

Brandon watched in mild awe as the investigators went about their business. David walked up close to Brandon, looked at the old building and said, “Don’t worry. We’ll track this bastard down.”

“Yes, we will,” Brandon replied. “And if he has hurt Andrea in any way, I’m going to kill him.”

David heard Brandon’s words, but did not reply. There was no admonition of ‘No, don’t do that.’

CHAPTER TWELVE

The Investigation Goes Deeper

BRANDON DID NOT SLEEP FOR THE NEXT SEVERAL DAYS. Worse, all of his waking hours were spent in worry. So, he did not get any rest either physically or mentally. He finally reached a point where he was mumbling incoherently. Adding to the problem was that he had become unkempt. Brandon was normally a man who was clean shaven and freshly showered at all times, fastidious and demanding about wearing clean clothes.

Now, here was a man who had not shaved in many days and smelled like a garbage can. It was finally Don who decided to have a talk with Brandon and try to reach him for his own good.

"Brandon, you look like shit. You smell like shit too. You're not any good to anybody like this. I want you to imagine Andrea seeing you in this shape. Wherever she is, she needs for you to be on top of your game more than ever. Now, I'm going to take you in the house, shove your ass in that shower and the girls are going to scrub you down. Then, I've got some tonic here to help you sleep. I'm going to knock you out with, it. Hopefully, you'll get at least eight hours of wink and be a new person when you wake up."

Brandon just looked up at Don without resisting or commenting. It was unclear whether or not he even understood what Don was saying. Be that as it may, he allowed himself to be led into the house, where, true to his word, Don stripped him, with the help of the girls, walked him into the shower and left it up to the girls at that point to scrub the man until all the stink was gone.

After he had been towel dried, he was led to his bed and while he sat on the edge, Don gave him a large slug of his magic elixir. Then Brandon was laid down on the bed and covered up to his chest with clean sheets. His eyes rolled back into his head, and everyone surrounding the bed crept out as quietly as possible, closing the bedroom door behind them.

Brandon slept for a full twenty-four hours. When he awoke, he was a different person. Gone was the whipped puppy. In its place was the determined, man in control, man with a mission. The lord of the jungle Brandon that people were used to, had returned. He bathed, shaved, dressed in clean khaki safari shorts and shirt and emerged on the front deck of the house, coffee cup in one hand, cell phone in the other, making calls, kicking ass.

The first thing he did was call a meeting. He wanted everyone in attendance; Lorenzo and Leticia, Don and Mary, Doug Bennett was in Florida, so he would be added into the conference by video-phone. The girls and even all four jaguars were called into the circle. Brandon managed to get David Harkness on the phone and asked if he might join them. Something in Brandon's voice made David know he had better be part of that conference. So, within minutes, a helicopter landed on the beach in front of the house and David Harkness came bounding out, attired in long trousers and a guayavera shirt. He rushed across the sand to the stairs and a moment later was on the deck.

The first thing Brandon wanted was an update on everything anybody knew. This status report was given primarily by David Harkness. But then they had to shift gears and update the progress on construction. Appearances had to be as normal as possible.

As it turned out, the DEA as well as the FBI and Interpol knew very little, except that they now had a profile of Reggie's brother. His real name was Clarence Oswald Carlson, and he was known as a troublemaker on his home island of Jamaica. When he left that island, it didn't break anybody's heart. Nobody knew where he had gone, and nobody much gave a damn. They were just glad to be rid of him. But no sign had been seen of him since he departed, so that trail ended there, in Jamaica.

"In my opinion," Brandon said. "We should analyze not just his motives for doing this, but what he hopes to get out of it. He must want something besides revenge. What? Money? Most likely, but he hasn't contacted us yet. Power? That would certainly fit the pattern if he is anything like his brother. All of that voodoo horse shit was nothing more than a power trip, an ego explosion."

"So," David said. "In your opinion, wherever he is right now, he's getting a big laugh out of this just because he thinks he's got one up on us? He's 'in control'?"

"Most likely," Brandon agreed.

"You know, it's easier to understand kidnapping for greed," David said thoughtfully. "People who want to collect money for somebody's life. But this ego stuff goes beyond something simple. Even something like revenge. This guy sounds like he's a couple of avocados shy of a guacamole. If that's true, it's gonna be more difficult to predict what he might do next."

"Not really," Brandon countered. "We need to calculate every move he will make being inspired by ego. What can he dream up that will satisfy *that* hunger?"

"How could anything satisfy that hunger unless he knew what we are thinking? What we are doing," David Harkness said.

Brandon locked eyes with David Harkness. "Of course! An inside informant? That absolutely makes sense. But who?" Then he looked at Lorenzo. "What we have going for us is that whoever this asshole is, he doesn't know we've broken the code. First of all, I want all of you right here committed to absolute secrecy. Everything that is discussed here, stays here."

The entire crew absolutely agreed. No swearing of loyalty was necessary.

"Now, Lorenzo, I want you to 'casually' observe the actions of every swinging dick on that construction crew. Get into conversations with them. Notice if they have anything new that costs money; new clothes, a new machete, a new hat, anything. I especially want you to watch that shrunk up little cocksucker, Adan. I have never liked him. I want to know if my instincts are right, and they usually are."

"Adan? Oh, come on Jefe. He's just a stupid little piss-ant farm boy. A campocino."

"Probably. But do as I ask anyway. His naiveté might just play right into the hands of Mr. Carlson the second."

"No problem!"

Brandon sighed. "I… I don't like this feeling of being so frapping helpless. I'm out of my league. I'm no investigator."

"Perhaps not," David Harkness said. "One man cannot be all things. But for what it's worth, we have some top-notch investigators working on this, including some that are under cover in Jamaica. Anyway, part of investigation is what we call, 'extrapolation', figuring out what the perp is thinking. Looks like you're doing a pretty good job at that."

"You think he'll go back there?"

"Where? To Jamaica?"

"Yeah."

"Maybe. Maybe not. But we have people working deep inside his circle of friends and family to learn more about him. We'll catch this punk. You can count on that. Nobody messes with one of our own and gets away with it. And in this case, I am taking it very personally. Andrea was my agent. She was also my friend. She still is."

"Do you think she's still alive?" Brandon asked, looking down at the deck.

"Don't even think like that. Goddammit, man! Of course, she's alive. This jerk needs her alive. She's his ace-in-the-hole. Right now, his plan is to use her to get revenge against you. In order to do that, she absolutely has to be alive. All we have to do is make him think his plan is working."

Brandon walked to the deck railing and looked out at the blue water of the Caribbean. Speaking to no one in particular, he said, "I'm going to kill that mother fucker."

All four jaguars gathered around him as if protecting him from some invisible enemy. And in fact, Brandon turned to them and spoke in a language no one understood, except Brandon and the jaguars. But when he finished speaking, all four cats broke loose with tremendous roars which did not abate for more than five minutes. The thunderous sound of the jaguars scared the hell out of everybody. Everybody that is, except Brandon.

"This woman gave me my life back. Now, she is my life." Brandon Shaw was sitting on a horizontal trunk of a coconut palm, down the beach a few hundred yards from the new house. His only companions were the four jaguars; Naja, Cisco, and the two cubs. They surrounded the man completely. But it was not them he was talking to. It was God.

"I realize I haven't lived my life according to your law, and I apologize for that. Maybe I don't have any favors coming, but I'm asking for one anyway. Please keep my woman safe until I can find her and rescue her from that incredibly crazy, asshole sonofabitch. In Jesus's name I pray, Amen."

And then, to the gathering of jaguars, he said in their secret language, "I'm going to need your help when we find her." Then Brandon stood up and began walking back toward the house. The jaguars marched beside him, knowing somehow, they were integral in this mission.

When Brandon arrived at the house, Lorenzo was waiting for him. "I need to tell you something, Jefe," Lorenzo said. "I think you may be right. Pinché Adan might be the rotten egg."

"What do you mean?"

"He's carrying a cell phone. It looks like an expensive one. He makes three Limps a day. How the fuck is he going to afford a cell phone? And besides, who would he call? He doesn't know anybody else that has a cell phone. He's a campocino Indian for crying out loud! Everybody he knows lives in a stick hut that doesn't even have electricity."

"Good work, Lorenzo! Let's call Harkness and fill him in."

"Why you wanna do that?" Lorenzo asked. "If you get the pinché fed here, he'll want to be going 'by the book'. I think we can find out what we want to know a lot quicker and easier."

Brandon looked at Lorenzo and smiled. "Get that campocino sonofabitch up here, on the deck, front and center. I'll have a little talk with Naja while you're doing that."

Lorenzo smiled and took off down the stairs as fast as he could go. "This is going to be pinché fun," he said, laughing.

Within a few minutes, Lorenzo returned, leading a very confused Adan up the stairs, onto the deck where Brandon awaited them, accompanied by four jaguars. Brandon Shaw sat comfortably, legs crossed, in a chair adjacent to the large square table. Surrounding him were four jaguars including Naja who looked at Adan unblinking with her golden eyes. Her black fur glistened in the sun.

Now, standing before Brandon, Adan seemed nervous. Brandon told Lorenzo, in English, to seize Adan's cell phone. Since Adan spoke no English, he didn't understand what was about to happen. Lorenzo reached inside a small shoulder bag that Adan carried and grabbed the cell phone, then handed it to Brandon.

Brandon looked at the expensive cell phone, then at Adan and asked, "Where did you get this cell phone?"

"I found it," Adan lied.

Brandon looked at Adan sternly. "Adan, I need information and I'm not in the mood to fuck around. You *are* going to tell me the truth. Now where did you get this phone?"

Adan froze, said nothing. Brandon said something to Naja, and Naja approached Adan, growled and raised up, then placed her huge paws on Adan's shoulders where she looked him in the eye from scant inches away.

"Adan, are you familiar with a jaguar's method of

killing? They take an animal's head in their mouth, say for instance a burro, then bite down until the skull pops. I've actually seen it a couple of times. There is a kind of sickening sound when the skull bone gives way. Then, there's all of that blood. It's messy as hell.

"Now," Brandon said. "If I give Naja the command, she's going to have your head for breakfast, then turn what's left of you into thick sliced bacon. Your family will never know what happened to you, because there won't be enough of you left to find. So, I'll ask you one more time. Where did you get this fucking cell phone?"

Adan was shaking violently. "Get her off of me."

"Not until you answer my question," Brandon said very calmly.

"That black man gave it to me."

"What black man?"

"The one from another country."

"Okay, now we are getting somewhere. Naja, anja kish!"

Naja immediately lowered her front quarters back down to the deck and backed off.

"Wise decision," Brandon said to Adan. "Whether you know it or not, you were moments away from dying. If you had answered my question with a lie, you would already be dead. Now, sit down, Adan. You are going to tell me everything, and I do mean everything, or Naja is going to finish what she started. Lorenzo, have Suyapa get a cup of coffee for Adan."

Lorenzo motioned to the girls who had been watching this scene play out from inside the glass patio doors.

"This black guy we're talking about," Brandon continued, "has kidnapped Doña Andrea. I need information to rescue her. Do you understand?"

Adan shook his head yes and managed a "Si, Señor,"

but he was shaking so hard that he was about to lose control.

"Okay. Start from the beginning. Tell me everything and don't leave any detail out. If you lie to me, even a little lie, you will die right there in the chair where you are sitting. Understand?"

Again, Adan nodded.

"Good," Brandon said. "Begin."

Adan said that one day when he was cleaning up the beach after a party, the Jamaican walked up to him and asked if he would like to make a lot of money. Adan asked what it was he had to do. The Jamaican said to meet him in Sambala at the old defunct temple, and he would explain everything. That's when it began.

Reggie's brother told Adan that he needed to know all the goings on at Jungle Cargo and even see an occasional picture, especially of Andrea and Brandon. He needed to know Andrea's schedule. Then he meticulously taught Adan how to use the cell phone and told him to never let anyone see him with it. But Adan was careless, and Lorenzo saw the phone.

Since Andrea's abduction, the Jamaican had been in touch frequently, wanting to know Brandon's responses, and everything that was going on almost hour by hour at the compound. His lust for TMI (too much information) was now the downfall of Adan, the conspirator.

Suyapa brought the coffee, then stood by close enough to overhear. At one point, she couldn't contain her anger and rushed forward, calling Adan every form of filth, then slapped him as hard as she could. "Desgraciado!" she yelled as she struck him. "Hijo de chingada! These people give you an honest job and treat you well. And you return their goodness with evil! You'll die in hell!"

Adan was shaking so hard that any hope of sipping the

coffee was lost. And now the left side of his face was turning scarlet where Suyapa had slapped him. Brandon picked up his own cell phone and called David Harkness. He filled David in with a sketch of what was taking place, to which David responded, "I'll be right there."

While they waited, Brandon said to Adan, "It's a stupid thing you did. You've pretty well fucked yourself, even in Sambala. You'll be an outcast there now, maybe even murdered in your sleep. And all for a few Limpiras. You are a pendejo, Adan. And oh, by the way, you're fired. Don't expect any severance pay. Chances are, you won't need any where you're going anyway."

"What do you mean?" Adan asked.

"Conspiracy to a kidnapping is a federal crime, even in Honduras. Where you're going, small guys like you are taught to be girls. Oh, you're going to have fun!"

Lorenzo laughed, and Suyapa yelled, "You deserve it, traitor. I hope you choke to death on a dick!"

Brandon looked around at Suyapa. He had never heard her say anything even remotely vulgar until now. This language was a barometer of her anger.

Moments later, a helicopter could be heard approaching. A minute later, and it was landing on the beach in front of the new house. David came springing out the bay door and sprinted toward the deck. He took the steps three at a time. Seconds later, he was unlatching the gate and entering.

Looking at Adan, he said, "Is this him?"

"Meet Adan," Bandon said. "Otherwise known as Benedict Arnold. He's a spy for Mr. Carlson of 'Jah-may-cah, mahn'!"

Brandon spent the next quarter of an hour relating what had transpired, leaving out the part about Naja 'encouraging' Adan to talk.

"How did you get on to him?" David asked.

"Lorenzo. He saw him with a cell phone, figured it was out of place. What does a campocino have use for with a cell phone? Reported it to me. We got him up here and encouraged him to spill the beans."

"How did you 'encourage' him? No, wait. I don't want to know. I imagine it's better the U.S. Government doesn't know either. Okay, good work. And kudos to you, Lorenzo."

"What is a kudo?" Lorenzo asked.

"A compliment," Brandon answered.

"Oh, I thought it was a horned animal from Africa," Lorenzo said with a smile.

"That's a kudu," Brandon retorted. "Are you fucking around with me?"

"Yeah," Lorenzo admitted, laughing a small laugh. "Hey, Mr. Harkness, thanks for the 'kudo'!"

"You're welcome," David said. "Okay, so we have the spy. We have the cell phone. What we need is a plan. There is a standard protocol for this kind of thing, but I don't think that is going to apply here. Tell you what, let this asshole bake in the sun for a while," he indicated Adan. "Let's go inside for some privacy, as well as some air conditioning, and talk. Whatever we do is going to take some extremely careful planning."

As everyone headed for the patio doors, Brandon turned and said to Adan, "Don't you move. If you try to get up from that chair, Naja will end your miserable, puke life."

If anyone was as angry as Brandon, it was David Harkness. "I don't like this side of myself," he said. "I'd like to kill some people, starting with that little dried up turd sitting out there on the deck. But… can't do that. Anger clouds your reasoning ability. We all need to stay calm, as cool as cucumbers. That way, we can put together a plan to free Andrea from this mess. But I've gotta tell you, when we have her safe, in our custody, I might take this badge off for a little while. I've never done it before, but Andrea is like a sister to me."

Brandon advisedly listened but said nothing.

"Having that cell phone is going to give us a leg up on finding Mr. Carlson the Second."

"How's that?" Brandon asked.

"To start with, our campocino spy out there probably called only one number. There's a chance we can find out who that number is registered to and where he gets his mail. But that's just the beginning. All cell towers have a registry. We have the phone. We are now in control. When this phone makes a call, the computer will tell us exactly where the call went to."

"That sounds too simple."

"There's really nothing simple about it. And people like the second Mr. Carlson who probably knows nothing about electronics, doesn't realize he is throwing a net over his own head by using cell phones. Let's go have a brief chat with our shrunk up little dog turd, Adan."

David rose and walked out onto the deck, followed by Brandon, Don and Lorenzo. David approached Adan.

"Tell me, Adan, did you use any kind of a special signal when you called the Jamaican? Did you let the phone ring once, twice and then hang up? Anything like that?"

Adan shook his head. "No, Señor."

"Alright," David said and then started to turn away. Suddenly, Adan jumped up from his chair and leaped over the gate by the steps. He scrambled down the steps and tripped at the bottom. Despite getting up quickly and running, it was futile. Brandon had turned away and didn't see what was happening in time. Naja, followed by the other three jaguars all went over the gate right behind Adan.

It was over before there was any time to stop it. Adan screamed as he was being attacked by all four jaguars and disemboweled right there in the front yard. It was a bloody mess. Looking over the railing at the scene below, David Harkness blanched.

"I remember a day when I thought that might happen to me," he said.

"But it didn't," Brandon said as he put one hand on David's shoulder.

"Never-the-less, I'll never forget it. I didn't sleep for a week after that. I didn't stop shaking for a month. Didn't stop shitting for three months! Now, seeing what might have happened… Lord!"

"What do we do now?"

"About Adan? I've got to call in a crew to take pictures, investigate, what not. He was essentially a suspect in custody and tried to escape. They'll investigate and then haul off the stiff. Return him to his family in Sambala at some point."

"No autopsy?"

"What for? This is Honduras. Andrea once told me you have a phrase for things like this. I think she said, 'Un incidente de la selva'. An incident of the jungle! Is that right? The only thing we need to do now is hope that Adan was the only rotten apple in the barrel."

"Aye, chingow!" Lorenzo said. "There had better not be any more fleas on this dog."

"In any case, we had better act fast," David said. "You know, I have an idea. We'll have a meat wagon that has to come out here to take away the pieces of the late Mr. Adan. While the ambulance is here, we're going to take advantage of it for a photo-op."

"What?" Brandon asked.

"Here's my idea," David said, and then explained what he had in mind to the three men surrounding him.

A couple of hours later, an ambulance from La Ceiba was backed up to the door of the new house, the back doors open, loading a very pale looking Brandon Shaw aboard. He was strapped to a gurney, eyes closed as if possibly unconscious. Someone standing nearby took a picture of this scene.

A second later, David Harkness said, "Good! We've got it. You can get up now."

Brandon asked the ambulance drivers to hurry and undo the safety straps, then he pushed the sheet aside and jumped off the gurney. "Let me see the picture," he said. David turned the phone toward him so he could see himself.

"Ooowheee! I look like refried dog dodo. Somebody hand me a towel so I can wipe this makeup off."

"Okay," David said. "Not a minute to waste. Let's send this picture to the number listed on the phone, 'sans comment' and see how long it takes for somebody to call and start asking questions."

David pressed the appropriate buttons and moments later, the photo was somewhere in cyber-space, en route to a destination as yet unknown. But hopefully that would quickly change. All the preparations had been made for electronic tracking. And because this was a kidnapping, the FBI was also heavily involved.

An hour passed, then two. And then, the phone rang. The ringer was set on 'vibrate only'. The plan had been carefully discussed. Lorenzo answered in a whisper voice.

"Bueno?"

A voice on the phone said, "I got the picture. What's going on there?"

"Don Brandon is very sick. He may have a heart attack."

"Oh yeah? Serves the son of a bitch right. Okay, you did good."

"Bueno. What now?" Again, in a whisper.

"How many people are left at Cuyamel?"

"Hardly anybody. Everybody is at the hospital with Don Brandon. Just the two maids are here."

"Perfect. I think this is the ideal time to come burn that whole fucking place to the ground." Then the voice on the phone hung up. The connection was broken.

Lorenzo looked at the phone, offended. "'Burn the whole place to the ground'? That pinché pendejo thinks he is going to burn our beautiful new conservatory to the ground? Not while I'm alive!"

"Okay, we're ahead of the game because now we know what this guy's plan is. And it's kind of stupid." David said.

"What do you mean?" Don Houseman asked.

"He's already committed one major felony, and a federal one at that, kidnapping. Now, he wants to return to the scene of the crime, so to speak, so he can exact some kind of demented revenge? He really is nuts." David looked at Brandon. "You said this brother of his, Reggie, was a squirrel? Idiocy must run in the family.

"So, we know he's coming. Two factors are missing. We don't know when, and we don't know how or from what direction. We've got to form contingency plans. Just like General Patton, we have to change the element of surprise to our side. And I've got to keep a cool head, which isn't going to be easy. All my life I've focused on being very professional, dispassionate, one step removed from whatever it was. But this time it's personal. I want that sonofabitch, and I want him like I have never wanted anybody."

"Bueno." Lorenzo offered. "We do know one thing. We know he's coming very soon, because he'll want to get here while he thinks Don Brandon is still in the hospital."

"That's true," Don said. "Good observation, Lorenzo. It would sure help if we knew how, which in this case is the same thing as where."

The men were standing on the new deck. A pandemonium of perhaps two hundred or more yellow naped amazon parrots flew down off the mountain-side, dipped low over the house making all sorts of racket, then continued straight on, out toward the sea. Brandon watched them, knowing they would have to turn at some point, but curious about how far they would go.

That's when he saw the large super tanker a few miles offshore, on the near side of the Cayos Cochinos Islands. The monster ship was headed west but surrounded and escorted by a squadron of four armed escort boats. Brandon wondered what a super tanker was doing taking this route instead of going north, directly across the Caribbean to the gulf. Was this some kind of a dodge to outfox Caribbean pirates which had become a plague? He went into the house, re-emerging quickly with a set of binoculars to get a better look. The four jaguars suddenly crowded very close to Brandon and seemed to be awaiting some instruction from him. The animals were definitely on alert, even to the point of the hair being raised on the nape of their necks.

As he stood at the railing, watching the distant boats, he said, "He's coming at us from the water."

"What?" Lorenzo asked.

"The bozo is coming at us from the water. He is

apparently obsessed with starting some kind of fire. If you were going to start a conflagration, wouldn't you want to arrive by, and escape via the sea? Besides, this guy is from Jamaica, an island that is surrounded by the sea. He's probably been on the water all his life. He'll come at us from the sea and plans to escape by sea."

"Just how sure are you about this hunch?" David asked.

"I'd bet my life on it," Brandon answered calmly.

"He may come at us from the sea," David said. "But that piss-ant isn't escaping anywhere. I'm gonna slap handcuffs on him so tight that he'll be screaming bloody murder all the way to the slammer."

"We've got to take him alive," Brandon cautioned. "There's no way he will have Andrea with him. I've got to get that information out of him before anything else happens to him."

David, standing very close to Brandon's side and staring at his profile as Brandon looked at the blue Caribbean said, "Yes, we've got to take him alive. And *keep* him alive. Right?"

"Most likely," Brandon answered.

Within an hour, David Harkness had six of his most highly trained and experienced agents in a tight huddle going over finite contingency plans, along with Brandon, Lorenzo and Don. The jaguars were there too, which was more than a little upsetting to the agents who had just arrived. But David tried to explain that Brandon and Lorenzo had complete control of the jungle animals. This explanation seemed to help some, but not much!

A separate part of that plan involved one of those Armed Escort boats. David happened to know the owner of the company and had made arrangements for help from the space-age guardians on the sea.

Meanwhile, the girls, as well as Mary, were in the house overhearing what was going on but were basically exempt from what was to come. They did however have specific instructions about what to do if Andrea was with Oswald Carlson, and if she was rescued. Once everything was in place, all they could do was wait.

Hiding places were carefully selected. For the jaguars, that part was easy. They would be glued to Brandon, and in the case of Cisco, glued to Lorenzo. But jaguars hide easily.

About an hour before sunset, David's walkie talkie crackled to life.

"Deacon Five, this is airborne recon. There's a boat headed straight toward Cuyamel from the Cayos Cochinos Cays."

"How big is the craft?" David asked.

"Can't get too close. Don't want to spook whoever is on board, but she looks to be about 50 feet, a power boat, catamaran hull; the kind that's popular with scuba divers. It's also the kind of craft they use most often for beaching, so yachters can throw wild parties in remote places."

"Good work! Thank you," David said.

Brandon grabbed his binoculars and walked to the deck railing. Peering through the glasses, it only took him a minute to spot them.

"I see them. Shit! They're almost on top of us. They'll hit the beach in less than fifteen minutes!"

"Everyone to their assigned places," David shouted. "It's show time!" He then alerted the crew aboard the armed escort boat that had been standing by, waiting precisely for this moment. Oswald Carlson was closing in on the perfect trap, set just for him.

In the final minutes, Lorenzo ran upstairs to alert the

body-guards from Sambala of what was on the brink of happening. "Keep these women surrounded, and guard them with your very life," he said, then scrambled back down the steps to resume his hiding place.

Several minutes later, the large catamaran eased up onto the beach in front of the new house. It was now obvious what Oswald Carlson had been doing on the beach all those times that he had been spotted. He was doing recon in preparation for a beach landing. He had been plotting this for quite a while. If that was the case, just how much careful planning had gone into his scheme? That is to say, just how treacherous a plotter was Oswald Carlson? The moment of truth had arrived.

Five men including Oswald gathered on the bow of the catamaran. They visually searched the entire area for any sign of life or any activity that would suggest a trap. But from their perspective, Jungle Cargo looked abandoned. Taking an extra precaution, Oswald Carlson took a small spy glass from his pocket, extended it and searched through it for any evidence of Brandon Shaw. Try as he might, he saw nothing. He said something to the men gathered with him on the bow of the catamaran and they retreated toward the stern, returning a moment later with red, plastic gasoline cans, that seemed to be full.

Since the criminal contingent on board the catamaran had their attention so riveted on the peaceful scene before them, they didn't notice the armed escort boat, armed to the teeth, stealthily approaching from directly behind them.

It was precisely at that moment that Andrea suddenly appeared on the deck of the catamaran. Her hands seemed to be tied behind her. Nevertheless, she ran as fast as she could and intentionally body slammed herself into Oswald Carlson, knocking him forward and overboard where he landed with a splash in the shallow water. Andrea then struggled to her feet and jumped overboard, landing next to Oswald. As she struggled to get on her feet and run, Carlson tried to grab her, but she kicked him hard, in the face, then turned and ran toward the house.

At this point everyone on the Jungle Cargo force broke cover and started running toward the catamaran. Andrea spotted Brandon and screamed at the top of her voice, "Brandon!"

Two of the men on the bow of the boat began shooting at Andrea. Oswald Carlson, holding his broken nose with one hand, reached into his beltline with the other hand and withdrew an automatic pistol, he took aim and shot Andrea in the back. She had barely reached Brandon, when she collapsed in his arms with a cry of pain, then fell unconscious.

This triggered something that no one had ever witnessed, and no one has spoken of since the moment it happened. And that includes, no one has had the courage to tell Andrea.

Brandon's eyes grew wide as he looked at his woman with fear that she might be dead. Then the eyes began turning the color of gold. A sound came from deep in his throat like that of a primal roar. It wasn't as if Brandon had control over this; for certainly, he did not. But it was indisputable evidence of his direct connection to the ancient legend he had tried so hard to deny and suppress. In this moment of fury, of unbridled rage, it released that spirit to take over his body. What were hands a moment ago were now massive, razor sharp claws.

Brandon was no longer Brandon. He was Báalam Máak, Jaguar Man, and this Jaguar Man was determined to exact revenge. Moments later, *five* furious jaguars closed in on a terrified Oswald Carlson, crossing the sand of the front yard in scant moments.

Carlson barely had time to scream his last scream of stark terror and agony before the cats reached him. They attacked in unison. There was a horrifying blend of roars as the enraged animals tore into Oswald Carlson. Naja took the man's head in her mouth and closed down like a two-thousand-pound vice. Oswald's skull made a sickening popping sound as it succumbed to Naja's Fury. Oswald Carlson was instantly dead.

By the time the jaguars finished with him, Oswald Carlson was unrecognizable as a human being. He was unrecognizable as anything. He had been ripped, torn and rendered into chunks of bloody flesh. A pool of blood washed back and forth around where the pieces of his body lay in the shallow water fronting the catamaran. And it had all been so fast, so very fast.

In the front yard, David Harkness, Don Houseman, Lorenzo and the federal agents stared open mouthed at the scene before them. Upstairs, in the house, Mary Thompson, flanked by bodyguards, watched through the patio doors.

The four remaining conspirators, still on the bow of the boat, ran in panic, eyes wide, toward the stern. Before anyone could stop them, the boat was put in reverse and withdrew in a roil of water from the beach into deep enough water to turn around.

David Harkness pulled his gun and fired several rounds at the catamaran, but to no avail. He then got on his walkie and said, "Escort boat, the men on board that craft have just killed a federal agent! Stop them!"

The catamaran turned and headed out to sea. The captain of the catamaran spotted the patrol boat and veered far to the east of the patrol boat's location. But it would take more than that. The armed escort boat was much faster than the catamaran and within a minute, it flanked the cat, whereupon the captain of the patrol boat commanded over the loudspeaker, "Halt in the name of the law and prepare to be boarded. You are under federal arrest!"

Several people on the catamaran made the not so wise decision to start shooting at the patrol boat with pistols and a machine gun. The patrol boat withdrew to a safe distance, and then obliterated the catamaran. Close to a dozen rapid-fire machine guns opened fire simultaneously, pouring thousands of rounds into the catamaran. The rounds from the patrol boat blanketed everything including hitting the gas cans on the bow of the catamaran which caused a huge explosion. Some pieces of the cat blew so high in the air that it took more than a minute for them to splash down into the fire on the surface of the water.

Brandon and David barely noticed. Brandon had once again returned to himself, and regained Andrea's side where he was cradling her in his arms. David was on his walkie, calling for a life flight helicopter. "Federal agent down! Federal agent down! Get that fucking Medevac helicopter here on the double!" He then got on his knees and reached around to Andrea's back to see what was binding her hands. It was only a plastic zip tie which he managed to cut very quickly.

Meanwhile, crew members aboard the armed escort boat were searching the wreckage offshore for signs of any survivors, but of course there were none. Everything, including humans had been vaporized in the explosion.

The four jaguars had taken up positions surrounding Andrea, and presented a formidable wall against all comers, excepting people they knew.

Andrea regained consciousness. She looked up into Brandon's face and said weakly, "Brandon, you're a mess. How did you get all that blood on you?"

"I'll never tell," he answered, with a wane smile.

Once the call was made for the life flight helicopter, David stared at Brandon and Andrea. He had walked a few steps away but turned and made his way back through the contingent of jaguars, then bent down and felt behind Andrea's back to see if he could locate the entry point of the bullet. It seemed to be on the left side. The good news was, Andrea was conscious and apparently coherent.

He knew the chopper would only take minutes to arrive. Meanwhile, he stood up and walked, staggering slightly, back through the jaguars again to where Don Houseman stood only a few feet away.

"What the hell did we just see here a few minutes ago?" David asked.

"What do you mean?" Don said.

"What do I mean? What do I mean? I mean, I, I, I saw a man turn into a fucking jaguar, team up with other jaguars and kill a perp, and then he *turned back into a man*! That's what I frigging mean! Either that or they need to take me away in a white coat. You saw it too, right?"

"I... don't have any idea what you're talking about," Don said, shaking his head slightly. "Which man are you talking about?"

"Aw, come on!" David moaned. "Goddammit! I just saw a..." There was a long pause. Then, "You know what? You must be right. I'm losing it. I'm slipping a cog. Some *strange* things happen around this place. I'm clearly out of my element. Tell you what... one time, I went looking for Brandon Shaw. I walked a little way to the east of here, though those woods just past your house, and all of a sudden, I was facing a whole goddamn row of jaguars. A *ROW* of them! I'm talking about, there must have been twenty or thirty. Jaguars! All of them were just sitting there. Jaguars, all in a row, looking at me, like they were sizing me up for an hors d'oeuvre. See, jaguars don't do that. Right? So, this is the same illusion, part two. Shit! Forget it! I need a drink!" David stomped off, up the stairs to the house where he knew there was liquor.

Don looked at Lorenzo. "You know what he's talking about?"

"Helllll no! I ain't seen nothing," Lorenzo said, shaking his head. "If there ain't no pictures of it, it didn't happen."

"I would have to agree with that. I would have to maintain, that is the best policy," Don said in agreement.

At that moment, the sound of an approaching helicopter could be heard. Brandon looked into the eyes of the woman he loved with all his heart and soul.

"Hang in there, Baby. Help is almost here. You're going to be fine."

"Stay with me, Brandon," Andrea said as a tear rolled down her cheek.

"Nothing on earth could make me leave your side. I'll be here for the rest of our lives. You have my oath." Andrea managed a smile. The chopper set down on the beach. Medics immediately scrambled out the bay doors with an emergency medical kit and a stretcher. Spotting the woman down, they ran to her. The jaguars growled and Brandon had to issue a command to them to part and allow the men through the cordon.

Moments later, they were taking her vitals, transmitting the information to the hospital, receiving instructions for on-site emergency treatment, and within minutes, she was on the chopper, headed for the hospital. Brandon, David, Don and Mary, Leticia and Lorenzo accompanied her.

CHAPTER THIRTEEN

The Hospital

In the waiting room just outside the ER, the four men, Leticia and Mary waited in chairs for some news from the doctor. Time ticked by slowly. Brandon, still wearing bloody clothes, never sat for more than a few minutes at a time. Then he would get out of his chair and pace, looking through the glass window in the door leading down the hall to the operating room.

Finally, an assistant who had been in the ER where the operation was taking place walked out through the doors en route to somewhere for something. Brandon blocked his way and stared at the man without speaking. There was no need to do so. The man knew what was wanted by everyone in the room.

"Look," he said. "I am not the head surgeon. He's the one that has to talk to you." Then he started to walk away, but Brandon grabbed him by the front of his green shirt and pressed him against the wall.

"We want to know what's going on," Brandon said in a tone that made his intention clear.

"The bullet is in there deep. It came 'close' to a lot of

things, the kidney, the liver, the lung. But it seems like Providence is on her side. We're just having to be extremely cautious while extracting it. Now let me go."

Brandon released the doctor's greens. The doctor looked Brandon over, up and down. "You're a mess," he said. "How did you get so bloody?"

"It's a long story," Brandon replied.

The doctor started to walk away, then turned. "Did anybody catch the thug that shot her?"

"We got him," Brandon said with finality.

"Good! I hope he's in jail," the doctor said as he walked away.

Brandon didn't respond. He just stood there. Finally, he looked down at himself.

"Sheesh! I really am a mess. I wonder if there are any stores still open? I need to grab some clothes."

Mary got up from her chair. "If you go out there, you're going to scare the hell out of people. I'll go find you some clothes. You need to talk these people into letting you use one of their showers. I'll be back by the time you're washed."

With that, Mary walked at a fast pace down the hall, and out of sight when she turned a corner.

Sure enough, by the time Brandon made arrangements for a shower and got scrubbed, Mary had returned with new clothes, which Don brought into the borrowed hospital room. They weren't exactly what Brandon would have chosen, but they were fresh and clean; checkered shorts and a sport shirt that looked like they belonged on a golf course.

Brandon chuckled when he saw them. "My new look!" he said, as he got dressed. When he returned to the seating area outside the ER, everybody managed a smile. Lorenzo grinned and said, "Chinelas, Jefe! I almost didn't recognize you."

At that moment, the head surgeon could be seen through the window in the door, walking toward them. Instinctively, everyone knew this was the moment they had been waiting for and rose from their seats.

When the doctor came through the doors, he removed his head gear and looked around at everybody. "Which one of you is her family?"

"We all are!" Everybody said in unison.

"Alright," the doctor continued. "Andrea is a very strong woman, and, a very lucky one. If that bullet would have hit one inch in any direction from where it did, it would have hit something, and we would be having a much different conversation.

"That said we got the bullet out. It's going to take some recovery time. She's going to need a lot of rest, but she'll be fine."

"What about the baby?" Mary asked.

"Like I said, nothing of any importance was hit, least of all her uterus. As long as she takes care of herself and gives this wound time to heal, the baby will be fine."

There was a collective sigh of relief. The doctor shook hands with everybody, and then said, "Which one of you is Brandon?"

"I am," Brandon said.

"This is for you!" The doctor handed Brandon a piece of gauze bandage with something wrapped in it, then he walked away. Brandon opened the bandage to find the bullet that had been removed from Andrea.

Brandon stared at the bullet. "I'm going to get this made into a pendant to wear around my neck. It will be a reminder to always watch over my woman more closely."

"I just hope that's the last of the Carlson's," Lorenzo said.

Another ER worker came to the doors and announced that Andrea was in recovery.

"Are we going to be able to visit?" Mary asked.

"So long as you keep it very quiet," the nurse said. "She needs rest."

Everyone fairly tiptoed back to the recovery room and surrounded Andrea's bed. Brandon, standing to Andrea's left, bent over the bed and kissed his woman on the forehead.

An hour later, when Andrea began to awaken, she found herself surrounded by her Jungle Cargo family. She managed a smile. And then a thought hit her.

"The baby?"

"The baby is fine," Brandon said. "And so are you. They dug a nine-millimeter slug out of you that managed to miss every vital organ. It's a miracle. I'm starting to believe in miracles!"

"So, I'm going to recover?"

"One hundred percent. The doc says you just need lots of rest."

"Oh, Brandon! Take me home. You've got to get me out of this hospital. I hate hospitals."

"Well, I share your sentiments for sure. But that doctor isn't about to let you out of here for a few days. This isn't a rash you're dealing with. You've been shot!"

"Ohhh! Did you get him?"

"Who?"

"Carlson, that frimp!"

"Yeah, we got him."

"Thank God. He's as weird as his brother. No, *more weird*." She looked at David. "He'll do a lot of time in the feds, right?"

"Actually, no. That isn't a consideration any longer."

"Why not? He's broken at least three federal laws."

"Mr. Carlson isn't with us anymore."

Andrea looked at David, then at Brandon. "Was it you?"

Brandon glanced at everyone in the recovery room, as if to say, 'No one breathe a word.' Then, he looked into Andrea's deep blue eyes. "I had help. Me, Naja, Cisco… the two cubs."

Andrea looked straight at David. "Oh. I think I understand. Served the sonofabitch right," she said.

You could see the anger in her expression. Then she visualized the attack. "I'll bet he was a mess," she said, totally without emotion. This was so unlike Andrea that it immediately made everyone present suspect what Oswald Carlson had done to Andrea while she was his prisoner.

Andrea was in the hospital for a week. During that time, Brandon Shaw did not leave her side, not even for a moment. She was placed in a private room that was the size of a suite. Brandon had a cot brought in and slept next to her hospital bed. He showered and shaved in the hospital room bathroom and had meals catered from the restaurant down the street. He absolutely refused to eat hospital food, saying it tasted like cardboard. But no matter, he was cleaved to his woman and it would have taken an army to pull him away. The hospital staff knew it and just accepted it as a matter of course.

During this time, David Harkness spear headed an official investigation into the incident. This included a raid on Oswald Carlson's presumed 'headquarters' in the Cayos Cochinos Islands. That house and grounds were gone over intensely with a fine-toothed comb. The entire house was dusted for fingerprints to hopefully identify any other people associated with Carlson. David Harkness conducted the investigation with a vengeance. Fury could be seen in his expression by anyone standing close to him.

"If you see so much as a flea in this house, I want it interviewed," he said in a voice that was near yelling. And then more to himself than anyone around him, he mumbled, "If I find any other mother fucker that was a part of Andrea's abduction, I will personally see to it that he dies of old age in prison."

Meanwhile, at Jungle Cargo, Don Houseman with Lorenzo Ponce acting as his manager, was progressing rapidly with the new construction, and it was going exceedingly well. As it came together, he viewed it one day from a new drone he had purchased, and said to everyone gathered around the computer screen, "And that maniac wanted to burn this beautiful place to the ground!"

"Hijo de la chingada!" Lorenzo added.

At last, the office was completed. This building was situated between the old and the new houses at Jungle Cargo. Not only was it built atop pilings, like all of the buildings were at Cuyamel, but this one had a second story. In typical Don Houseman fashion, it was built strong, with tropical storms and even an occasional hurricane in mind.

Then came the day that Andrea would be caged up in a hospital room no more. Even having Brandon at her side did not ameliorate her sentiments.

"One more minute in this place and I'm going to scream," she said, obviously frazzled, and pulling at her flowered hospital gown. "Brandon, please get me out of here this minute and take me home. I cannot stand one more second of this stupid hospital rag that opens up and exposes my butt every time I get out of bed. It's demeaning! When I go to the bathroom, I have to drag this thingamajig with a baggie and tube stabbed into my arm." You ever try to clean yourself after using the bathroom with one of these needles in you? It's completely undignified!

"I want to be surrounded by *my* things, in *my* house, by people who I know. I even want the cubs near me, pests that they are. And I also want some real food. I want Anna Maria's cooking. I'm going to go crazy in here."

"I've already got your release papers," Brandon said with a smile. "Surprise, surprise! Here's a clean set of clothes for you. Just wait for the nurse to unhook you from that gizmo."

He handed her the complete set of clothing including shoes. Andrea immediately sat on the side of the bed and started hitting the buzzer to call the nurse. Minutes later, the nurse had removed the painful "intravenous port." Thus freed, Andrea climbed quickly into her clothes. She couldn't move fast, but she moved with determination.

Another nurse arrived with a wheelchair and Andrea fairly hopped into it. "Whatever it takes to get out of this place," she said. "Please, let's just go."

There is no way Brandon was going to travel the nightmare, pothole riddled road from La Ceiba to Cuyamel. So, he drove to the heliport, adjacent to the La Ceiba Airport and hired a chopper.

He could tell that Andrea was in quite a bit of pain by the way she moved when she got out of the Jeep and walked to the chopper, then struggled to climb aboard. But he also knew that nothing this side of hell was going to stop her. She wanted to go home. So, once they were airborne, Brandon called ahead to the house, advising everyone they were on their way and to arrange a sedate reception for the returning Andrea.

When the chopper landed on the beach at Cuyamel,

everyone was waiting; Lorenzo, Leticia, Don, Mary, all four jaguars. As soon as the chopper was down, everyone rushed toward the aircraft to greet Andrea and give her whatever assistance she needed in getting down from the helicopter, then up the stairs to the house.

Even though the day was mild by Honduran standards, Andrea did not want to sit in a chair on the deck. She needed the cooler temperatures inside the house, in the air conditioning.

She refused to be in a bed any longer, having spent a full week bedridden, she had had enough of beds. Instead, she propped herself up on the new sofa that had electric head and foot-rests. She allowed her lap to be covered with a light blanket. The girls brought her tea. Then she wanted Leticia and Mary to bring her up to date with anything and everything having transpired during her absence.

CHAPTER FOURTEEN

A Dark Cloud Passes

"All I want to do is put the past few weeks behind me. I can't pretend they didn't happen, but I also can't pretend I feel bad about Mr. Oswald Carlson taking the big hickey. He was the worst kind of pervert and he needed to be dead a long time ago. Now, before we were all so rudely interrupted, we were planning a triple wedding. I suggest we continue doing that and look ahead instead of looking back. Now, let's get on with what is important."

Andrea was addressing everyone in the inner circle, who were gathered around her as she sat on the new sofa. At the end of her short speech they looked at one another, then back at her. There was something a little different about Andrea. Brandon thought it was anger she was feeling toward the late Oswald Carlson. It was clear that Andrea didn't want to talk about it, but that bastard had done something to her, something horrible, and Brandon thought he knew what it was. If his suspicions were right, it made him even more glad that Carlson was dead, and just as glad that he had participated.

Meanwhile, the jaguar cubs had resumed their position

as bodyguards; and this time, Andrea welcomed them. She was just beginning to be at the moving around stage, but even when she went out onto the deck, she made sure she left the patio doors open long enough for the cubs to make their way through the doors and stay with her.

The upsetting thing to Brandon was that she didn't seem to need him as she usually did. He even commented to Don Houseman. "I'm worried about her. She is not herself."

Don agreed. "I know. Something is eating at her. You know, I have heard that sometimes victims of things like this have a tendency to blame themselves. I wonder if that's what's going on here?"

"What could Andrea blame herself for? It sure wasn't her idea to be kidnapped by some freak."

"Doesn't matter. They do it, anyway, thinking about things they might have done differently. Truth is, nobody knows what the future holds, even five minutes from now. That's what you're going to have to get across to her."

Time didn't help. Four days later, Brandon & Mary stood in the kitchen, looking out through the patio doors at Andrea, sitting in a chaise lounge, guarded by the cubs.

"By now, she should be moving like a juggernaut. We've got this mega-wedding to plan and she just says she isn't feeling up to it. Something is terribly wrong. I don't think anybody, but you can fix it, Brandon. And you need to fix it now. Don't wait a minute longer. If you do, she's going to sink deeper into that depression she's in, or whatever it is."

It wasn't that Brandon was out of patience, but his concern had peaked. He knew Mary was right, so he went outside, onto the deck to join Andrea.

"Mind if I join you?"

"Suit yourself." Andrea seemed distracted, distant.

"Wow! Those don't sound like the words of a woman who is about to get married."

Without looking at him, maintaining her gaze on the blue water beyond the beach, she replied, "There isn't any rush, is there?"

Brandon sat on the side of the chaise lounge so he could face Andrea. "Alright, enough. Lover, what I am about to say is coming from love. But you need to listen and listen really good. I can't be sure what's going on inside that pretty head of yours, because you haven't shared with me like you usually do. So, you can stop me when you think I've wandered too far-off track.

"What you're experiencing is not uncommon among survivors of things like kidnapping. I'm guessing there are two things bugging you. One, you're experiencing guilt because you feel that if only you had done something a little differently, it might not have happened. Let me just say, with all the love in the world, horse shit! That asshole plotted his attack for weeks, maybe even months. There was no way it was not going to happen. He *was* going to carry out his insidious plan, one way or another. If he hadn't caught you on the La Ceiba road, he would have gotten you somewhere else. He even had a spy working on the inside so he would know our every move."

Andrea blinked and finally looked at Brandon. "Who?"

"That little shrunk-up campocino turd that Lorenzo hired, Adan."

"Where is he now? I'd like to give him a piece of my mind."

"Not possible. He's joined Mister Carlson in the big sky. Well, in their cases, I doubt it's in the sky. The point is *nobody* messes with my lady!"

Andrea put her hand over her mouth at the news that Adan was dead.

"Okay, let's cut to the chase," Brandon said, more cautiously. "I'm guessing that heathen son of a whore did something unspeakable to you. Something you are afraid, or too ashamed to tell me about because you think it will affect our relationship, change the way I feel about you. So, let me repeat, horse shit!"

Brandon held up his hand. "Please, it is not necessary to confirm or deny it. What is necessary is for you to know that we are getting married. We have a son on the way. We have a new house that needs your touch. You and two other ladies have a wedding to finish planning. And here's the really good part; nothing that piece of shit might have done could possibly make me feel any differently about you, except for feeling more protective of you. Now, have we got that straight?"

Andrea smiled for the first time in many days. "When did you become such a philosopher, Mr. Shaw?"

"Well, I had a lot of input help from an older dude named Don Houseman. He is old, but very wise, the official Jungle Cargo guru. And if I could, I would adopt him as my brother."

"I see. And he taught you all of this?"

"No. Just some of it. But he has a way of priming the pump, so to speak."

"Priming the pump. Hmmm. Interesting. Well, I've enjoyed our little chat, sir, but I have a wedding to plan, and time's a wasting!"

With that, Andrea got up from her chaise lounge and went inside the house to join the two other women. Gone like magic was the looming dark shadow that threatened Andrea's positive attitude and sanity. Brandon smiled as he watched his woman rejoin life, and he silently thanked Don Houseman for his newfound wisdom.

CHAPTER FIFTEEN

Guess Who's Coming to Dinner?

CONSTRUCTION IS A FUNNY THING. WHEN A CREW IS IN THE throes of building something, it appears, from the outside looking in, that the project will never be finished. Building materials are scattered everywhere. There is the sound of electric saws and nail guns banging away. Plus, the voices of construction workers calling out measurements so the 'cutter' on the ground can saw a board to the precise length needed and hand it to a carpenter. Then too, there is the frequent expletive when a mistake is made, or something goes wrong. Essentially, it's a beehive and the fact that anything turns out the way it is supposed to is nothing short of a minor miracle.

Thus was the case at Jungle Cargo. The workers were divided up into several separate crews, each with an assigned task. But they were all running in different directions at the same time. To the casual observer, it looked like one giant game board of mayhem, squared by chaos; to say nothing of an ant mound. The fact that it all made any sense at all bordered on comedy.

But as with all well-organized construction jobs, the day

must come when the action winds down and reaches a successful conclusion. Such was the case with the remodeling of Jungle Cargo. The project had not only reached a successful conclusion, but it had done so ahead of schedule and below the predicted budget, all thanks to the knowledge and expertise of Don Houseman.

As Brandon, Lorenzo and Don walked the wide meandering path, performing an informal on-site inspection, Brandon could not believe his eyes. "A few short months ago, this was nothing but raw, tangled jungle," he said with pride. "Don, you are an amazing human being. I owe you."

"No," Don said with a smile. "It's me that owes you. As a person gets older, they feel their worth to the world has vaporized before their eyes. They feel like a relic, a leftover, in somebody's way. This project has given me my pride back. It gave me a chance to employ all of my experience and skills to create something beautiful. I am the one who is grateful. But I do have one suggestion."

"You have my attention," Brandon said.

"Lorenzo voiced some concern a while back about turning this place into a tourist attraction. I agree with him, and I disagree with him."

"How's that?" Brandon asked. By now, Lorenzo's ears were also perked up.

"In my opinion, you should allow people to come here. But they should not be allowed to just run around unsupervised. What I see here is a marvelous chance to inform and educate. Especially those young minds that are always so thirsty for new information and new ideas. I think you would be doing a huge service toward your ultimate goal by having strictly regulated guided tours through here. Arrange booking of schools and other organizations. Have trained guides lead them and talk about the jungle, the vital role that parrots play in the eco system; teach them something and charge for the service."

"Hijo!" Lorenzo said. "I never thought about that. That would work! Hell yeah, I would go along with that. Alternate tours. Have some in English, some in Spanish."

"Yes but wait! That's not all. Lorenzo is worried about control of visitors. It's a valid concern. But there's another concern. This meandering trail we have created extends well over a mile. That's an awful long distance for a family with children to walk. So, they shouldn't."

"What?" Brandon said.

Don smiled. "You know those open air golf kart type busses that run on electricity and carry a couple of dozen people at a time? We need two. One for Spanish tours, one for tours in English. Families stay together. The little ones don't get tired or overheated. We could install CD players in them and have CDs with all the information we want to impart to visitors. That way, nothing would ever be forgotten or left out because of boredom of repetition."

"Chinelas!" Lorenzo said with a whistle. "Don, you are a pinché genius. Hey wait! We would also need a gift shop. Every time I have gone some place on a tour of any kind, there was a gift shop where I could buy a souvenir for a requerdo."

Brandon looked at Don. "Are you willing to build one more building? You know, we do need restrooms in any case."

Don laughed. "It would be my pleasure."

"We could set up perimeters so that arriving visitors needed to go inside the gift shop to get their tickets. That would give them a good chance to see the gift shop and get buying ideas. The tours could begin and end at the same door going into the gift shop! I love it!" Brandon said excitedly.

And so, a location was selected for a gift shop. There would also be a need for barriers, trail-side signs, all the trappings to make it comfortable for visitors. So, a new project was begun. Granted, a much smaller project than the one just completed, but a project, never-the-less.

By now, Don knew who his best carpenters were. So, it would be easy to hire only those men in order to get the gift shop up as quickly as possible and to the highest quality possible. The three men went to the office to lay out a basic floor plan for the proposed structure.

Meanwhile, the three women of the inner circle had concluded their in-depth plans for the triple wedding and started ordering things and scheduling people. A date was set and to say there was excitement was an understatement. The air was absolutely electric.

However, there was still one thing left to do insofar as Andrea was concerned. She needed to call home to Indiana and fill her parents in on the events of her life for the past two years. She had been remiss in communicating with them because she was never quite sure how to describe Brandon Shaw. Now, she wasn't sure what kind of a reception she would get.

This wasn't going to be fun. So, Andrea fixed a big cold glass of guayavera juice and sat down at the big square table by herself to make the phone call. A half hour later, she got up and walked back into the house, to the kitchen, not looking happy. Mary Thompson was there, installing shelf paper in the cabinets for her friend. She saw the expression on Andrea's face.

"How did it go?" Mary asked.

"About like I expected, or a little worse," Andrea replied. "Mom wasn't there. She was out shopping. Dad vacillated back and forth between being angry and stoic."

"Are they coming to the wedding?"

"I doubt it. Honduras is a world away in their minds. It's hard to get them outside the city limits of Indianapolis. Well, I've done what I can. It's not in my hands anymore. We're going to press forward with this triple wedding. Damn the torpedoes, full speed ahead."

"Did you tell your father you are expecting?"

"Yeah. That's the part where he swallowed his tongue. My folks are mid-America, provincial. One does not get in a family way without a wedding ring on their finger. There is little more than a handshake before marriage and coitus is performed in the missionary position *only*, and probably no more than once a week, preferably on Wednesday night after church."

"Oh, dear. How did you ever escape that mindset?"

"I joined the DEA and then fell in love with a wild jungle man."

Mary laughed. "That sounds like a rather abbreviated version of things, but okay."

Andrea looked back out through the glass patio doors and sighed. "I really do wish they weren't so stiff necked. I'd love to have my father give me away, even though he isn't my real father. But... wishing and reality are seldom traveling companions. Let's move on."

Then Andrea thought of something. She picked up her phone and called the number of the phone she had given to Didier. Several rings later, much to her surprise, Didier answered.

"Hello?"

"Didier! This is Andrea."

"Andrea! How wonderful to hear your voice. How are you?"

"I'm fine. Didier, I have a favor to ask."

"For you, the moon and the stars. You have but to tell me what it is."

"I don't think my father is going to come to the wedding, and I need someone special to give me away. Didier, will you do me the honor?"

"You take my breath away. All I need to know is where and when."

Andrea smiled broadly as she filled Didier in on the details. By the time she ended the call, she felt much better.

Then Mary said, "But what if your father does come?"

"I don't think there's much of a chance of that. First, he'd have to pull that corncob out of his ass, and I think it's in there too deep. It's time to forget him and move on."

And 'moving on' is what they did. The wedding date had been set, and the countdown was on. A triple wedding was in the offering. By now, the event had gained enough momentum that nothing was going to stop it.

Several days passed, filled with multiple activities leading up to the wedding and reception. This including many 'in person' meetings with various people all the way from tuxedo renters to caterers. They even hired an 'exterior decorator' to pull the front yard into shape so it would look festive enough for the occasion. The 'exterior decorator even seemed to have one thing in-common with many interior decorators. He was light in the loafers.

Anybody who has ever lived in a beach house knows that front doors and back doors are reversed from that of conventional homes. The 'front' door is always the one facing the water. The 'back' door is the one facing the street, the parking lot, or in this case, the jungle. All of this is to say that two days before the wedding, there was a knock at the *back* door of the house.

Suyapa answered it to find a man and woman standing

there who looked a little lost and very much out of place. Both people were in their mid-sixties and dressed as if they were still in the United States. The man sported 'braces' to hold up his trousers with a pin striped, short sleeved shirt. The woman had grey hair styled in a short coif. She was dressed in a nice, but conservative flowered dress.

The woman said, "Where is my daughter?"

Suyapa said in Spanish, "I'm sorry. I do not understand."

The American woman said, "Andrea?"

Suyapa said, "Ah! Doña Andrea! Si." And then she said, "Pasalé, por favor." And motioned the couple inside. Then she ran quickly to the bedroom where Andrea, Mary and Leticia were doing final touches to their wedding dresses with the help of a seamstress from La Ceiba.

"A man and woman are here looking for you," Suyapa said to Andrea. Andrea's brow wrinkled slightly.

"A man and woman?" Andrea left the bedroom, still wearing her wedding dress, and, followed by Mary and Leticia, went to the parlor to see who had arrived. She almost fainted when she saw her mother and father standing there.

"Mom? Dad?"

"Hello, darling," her mother said as she moved toward Andrea to give her a hug. "When your father told me you had called... well, he's such an old grouch. There is no way either of us are going to miss our daughter's wedding."

Andrea was stunned and speechless. Now her father came to her for a hug. "Hello, Andrea. Surprise! I'm sorry I was such an old fart on the phone. I don't know what the matter was with me."

"Oh, my God!" Mary said.

"I know what the matter is with you!" Andrea's mother said. Then, looking around at the new house, added, "My goodness. This place is beautiful. When Tom said Honduras, I imagined you living in some grass shack on the beach."

"Well, we are on the beach," Andrea said, managing a smile.

"Yes, you certainly are." It was at that moment when Sarah Granger looked through the patio doors and saw four jaguars relaxing on the deck. Her face went pale and she staggered. Tom Granger managed to catch her and steady her. She raised a shaky finger and managed to point. "Oh, dear. It must be the heat. I think I'm seeing things."

Tom Granger looked toward whatever had upset his wife, then spotted the jaguars. "Oh, Jesus wept! What the hell are those things?"

"Those 'things' are called jaguars, Dad. They are our pets and our family. They belong here."

"Jaguars? Pets? You have jaguars for pets… loose, walking around, not in cages? I must be seeing things. It looks like there are at least four of them out there. Aren't you afraid they'll crash through those glass doors and attack you?"

"I don't think you heard me, Dad. They're very close pets, like a part of our family."

"Is the huge black one a jaguar too?"

"Yes. Her name is Naja. She is the mother of the two cubs. That other big one is Cisco. He's the father."

"Are those what you were referring to when you said you had four 'cats,' on the phone?"

"Yes, they are."

"I thought you meant… tabbies, or a Siamese. Never in my wildest dream!"

"Well Dad, I didn't think it made much difference because it didn't sound like you were coming to the wedding."

"Like your mother said, we wouldn't miss something this important in your life. Besides, I came here to forgive you."

Andrea's eyes immediately narrowed. "Forgive me? For what?"

Her father indicated her swollen stomach. "Well, I mean…"

"If that's why you came here, you can just turn around and go back to Indiana. I haven't done a damn thing to be 'forgiven' for. I'm not pregnant because of some one-night stand. I am pregnant by the man I love and have been in love with now for a couple of years." Her voice rose to near shrieking. "Don't you *dare* come here with that holier than thou attitude." Her hands were clenched into fists.

Andrea's parents stood wide eyed silent. They had no response because they had been put skillfully in check. This was not the daughter they knew from years ago who didn't know how to defend herself against such an attack. The person before them now was a woman, and not one to be trifled with.

It was at that moment that Brandon, Don and Lorenzo came up the stairs to the deck. They were engaged in chatter. All of them talking and laughing about the addition of the gift shop and how they now needed to look on the internet for an electric tour bus.

They opened the patio doors to come into the kitchen, and the cubs managed to slip inside with them. The cubs immediately went to Andrea, who was standing close to her parents. Her mother gasped and her father backed up a couple of steps.

Brandon was talking to Don and Lorenzo. "So, then the guy says, 'Oh, now I get it, you want *both* of them painted!'" The three men laughed. Brandon headed for the refrigerator.

"Hi honey," he said to Andrea. "We need something cold to drink. How are the last minute fittings going? That dress looks beautiful, by the way."

"Brandon," Andrea said. "I'd like to introduce you to my parents. This is Sarah and Tom Granger. Mom, Dad, this is Brandon Shaw, the man I'm going to marry."

Brandon closed the refrigerator door and walked toward Tom and Sarah Granger.

"Your folks? I'm honored. Glad to meet you." With that, Brandon stuck out his hand in greeting. The introductions and following get-to-know you chit chat went well. Andrea's parents had been put in their place and, realizing all the cards were on Andrea's side of the table, they kept any prejudices they might have held to themselves. Brandon also introduced Don and Lorenzo, who got their drinks, but kept a respectful distance while relationships were established between Brandon and his soon to be in laws.

After about twenty minutes, Brandon excused himself saying, "I know all of you have a lot of talking to do. And we need to get back to work."

"Yes," Tom said. "I saw all of that construction going on out there. What are you building?"

"Oh, that's a very long story," Brandon said. "But in short, a psittacine bird conservatory. Tell you what, when you get settled in, we'll take you for a tour and let you see it all, first hand."

"Wonderful!" Tom said. "I would enjoy that."

"Where's your luggage?"

"What? Oh, dear! It's downstairs, in the taxi. I forgot all about..."

"Don't worry," Brandon said. "I'll take care of the taxi and, Lorenzo, would you mind helping me with the luggage? Andrea, show them into the guest room of your choice."

With that, Brandon was out the back door and tromping down the steps, Lorenzo close at his heels. As Brandon disappeared down the steps, Tom Granger turned to his daughter and said, "I like him. He's a gentleman, but I can sense a real animal magnetism about him. Where did you meet him, Hon?"

"*That* is a long story, Dad. Too long for right now!"

And she left that right there... she hoped! Truth be told, she had mixed feelings about Tom Granger even being here. He wasn't her real father. Her blood father had died in Vietnam from a drug overdose. Tom Granger was just a paste-in-place her mother had married after her real father died. True, he had adopted her, and raised her. But she had never felt very close to him. In the back of her mind there was always the ghost image of her real father, whom she had loved with all her heart. Ah well, no matter. Nothing could change any of that now. She just looked upward and thought, *Forgive me, Pop. Nothing or nobody will ever take your place in my heart.*

Then, another thought hit her. She turned to Mary and said softly, "Oh good grief! Didier!"

"Exactly!" Mary replied.

"I've got to call him right away and try to explain," Andrea said as she walked toward the bedroom where her phone was lying on a bedside table. A minute later, Didier's number was ringing.

"Hello?"

"Didier, Andrea."

"Yes, I recognize your voice (laughter)."

"Didier, I have a problem. My parents have showed up from Indiana."

"Oh? Well, that takes a lot of pressure off. You want your father to give you away, right?"

"No, it's not right. I want you to give me away. But I'm sort of painted into a corner."

"Don't you fret about it for a second," Didier said. "I was worried about what to do anyway. I've never given anybody away before."

"Will you come to the wedding anyway? I want you there."

"I wouldn't miss it for anything in the world. Your father might give you away, but you are very much like a daughter to me. I'll be there."

When Andrea disconnected the call, Mary asked, "How did he take it?"

"Like the loving gentleman that he is. Have you ever met Didier?"

"No. But there have certainly been stories come out of the jungle about him. I'm looking forward to meeting him."

"You're going to love him. Here is a guy who was born in the middle of a mosquito infested jungle, to leper parents. Caught leprosy himself. Beat it, although he is badly scarred from it. Basically educated by a group of missionary nuns. Found a dream from reading a magazine, then made that dream come true, *in the middle of the jungle*! No experience, no money, no anything! Just imagination and heart. Lots and lots of heart. I admire him. I really do wish he was my father instead of that old fart-bag out there in the living-room."

CHAPTER SIXTEEN

The Great Convergence

DON'S IDEA OF USING TOUR VEHICLES WAS A GOOD ONE, BUT as it turned out, also an expensive one. The vehicles he referred to were called 'Twenty Passenger Electric Tour Carts' and the price tag was about fifty K each. A bit steep for a privately funded company that had just undergone a major construction project with subsequent bills to pay. So, the decision was made to order just one of the vehicles for the time being. Depending on how things went, another could be purchased later. Besides, ordering the one vehicle inspired costs other than merely the purchase price.

There would be freight and import charges, not to mention mordida (under the table money to officials). Don would also have to build a secure garage for the vehicle. Meanwhile, it would be easy to make one vehicle versatile and work for both English and Spanish tours just by changing the CD to the appropriate language. A ten second job at best!

This one topic ate up the first half of the day. Lunch was taken on the deck, with Andrea and her parents. Brandon had promised a tour of the grounds and project, and it was clear, Tom Granger was keen on seeing it. So, it was agreed that after lunch, the man and Andrea's mother would be given the cook's tour.

As it turned out, everybody wanted to go on the tour. Brandon warned those who had not been on this walk that it was arduous and hot. That deterred no one.

Tom Granger was duly impressed with everything he saw. "Wow!" was his most frequently used word, as the complete entourage walked the blacktop trail.

At one point, Brandon told Lorenzo, "It is now time for you to put the word out to all the hunters that we want birds. And this time, they don't have to cull the adult broncos the way they did previously. In fact, those are the main one's we want. That should mess with their minds! It's also time to get that bird expert down here from the San Antonio Zoo to train Mary. That is, if you still want that job?" He looked at Mary for a response.

"I've thought about little else for months," she said with a smile.

Brandon looked at Andrea. "Honey, would you please make the phone call? We're ready to get 'this bird' off the ground! Oh, Mary, we can't name the entire site 'The Bird's Nest'. It seems there are legal ramifications involving our Jungle Cargo permit that has to be grandfathered in. But we've decided to call the gift shop by that name. Do you like that idea?"

"Most definitely," Mary said, very pleased.

Tom Granger was hooked. He was deeply impressed by watching Brandon administrate. "This is a fantastic thing you're doing here. What do you think the revenue potential is for, what do you call it, Jungle Cargo?"

"There's no way to run a projection," Brandon said. "Nobody has ever done anything like this anywhere, much less in Honduras."

Suddenly, Andrea spoke up, and she sounded very firm. "We're not looking for an investor, Dad!"

Tom Granger became a little defensive. "Hey, it was just a question."

Brandon looked at Andrea but didn't dare say anything.

The tour wound down just in time. All of the ladies were beginning to tire, especially Andrea who was still recovering from a gunshot wound that she had conveniently overlooked telling her parents about. Brandon didn't press her about it. He figured she had her reasons.

However, when they got back to the house, as Andrea was lying down to rest in their bedroom, Brandon did ask her, "What was that about with your dad?"

Andrea had her forearm covering her eyes. "Believe me when I say, you do not want Tom Granger getting his hooks into you."

"Okay," Brandon said. "I'll take your word for it." He kissed her lightly on the lips. "Rest well. I've got things to check on." With that, he departed the bedroom, closing the door very lightly behind him.

When he arrived again at the display area, he found Lorenzo surrounded by six Indian hunters, all with cardboard boxes or burlap bags containing parrots. Lorenzo saw Brandon approaching.

"Oh, good, I'm glad you're here," Lorenzo said. "What is going to be the order for putting these parrots? That is, what kind of parrot goes in which flight cage?"

It was a good question. They had been so busy building the cages that no thought had been given to species assignment. So, the next hour was spent deciding which type of parrot would be the best neighbor to have in a cage adjacent to it. But the cages were divided so far apart, that it was dealer's choice.

Be that as it may, small identification signs had been

made for each cage. It was now time to attach them to the respective cages.

This was all the Indians needed to see. Now the word spread through the jungle like a wildfire that Jungle Cargo was all new, had dozens of more cages than ever before, and was buying all species of parrots and all ages. Hunters didn't have to cull the broncos. Within two days there were fifty hunters lined up in the morning with all kinds of improvised holding cages containing parrots. Lorenzo and Mary had their hands full just on the intake process. All this, and the wedding date was closing in on them, fast.

Decorators were let out of the gate to start decorating the wedding venue on the beach, and in the front yard, as well as the main deck where the reception would be held. Then, a last minute meeting was held with the caterers. There was no way that Suyapa and Anna Maria could handle this by themselves. Besides, Andrea had a special surprise in store for them.

Brandon had to gather the four jaguars around him and have a meaningful discussion with them because they were beginning to get nervous with all the new faces around. The last thing anyone would want is a 'nervous jaguar'. It was definitely not the same as having a nervous tabby!

Doug Bennet flew in from Florida and brought passengers with him. First was his wife, here to attend the wedding. But he also brought the bird expert to begin training Mary. And last but not least, he brought Rabbi Richard Goodman from Miami who was to perform the ceremony for Don and Mary. Although Mary would not be required to become Jewish to marry Don, she would have to undergo certain coaching in the Jewish marriage ceremony. Rabbi Goodman would be the houseguest of Don Houseman.

Doug hadn't seen the construction for several weeks now and it was nowhere at the stage it was when he left to go to Florida. He had to see it all, and after his inspection tour, it left him in open mouthed awe.

His wife, Francis, meanwhile, had joined the women in the house for unlimited 'pre-wedding nervous chatter'.

Brandon, Don, Doug and Lorenzo were holding a confab out on the deck when Brandon looked up at all the activity and said, "Good grief! This is really happening, isn't it?" Then he smiled broadly.

"Yes, it really is," Don agreed. "I didn't realize what I was starting when I decided to propose to that woman. It's like they're planning world war three in there!"

CHAPTER SEVENTEEN

The Ecumenical Triple Wedding

An overview of the wedding area could be best seen from the railing of the main deck. The 'aisle' would be a marked out path leading from the carport to the triple altar, which was on the beach in front of the house. That aisle would be flanked on both sides by decoratively covered folding chairs.

The altar itself would be comprised of three interconnecting arches, the mainstays of which were made from aluminum tubing, but festooned with coconut palm fronds and each bride's favorite flower: Mary's favorite flower was gardenias. Leticia loved roses and Andrea was passionate about orchids.

The three couples had all agreed that Don and Mary should be the first to take their vows. Brandon had been asked to be the best man not only for Don, but also for Lorenzo. And because Lorenzo had known Brandon for most of his life, Lorenzo had been asked to serve as Brandon's best man.

Lorenzo and Leticia would be the second couple to take their vows, Brandon and Andrea would be last, all based on the order in which the men proposed to their brides to be.

As for the ceremonies, Don and Mary would recite vows. Lorenzo and Leticia would have a standard ceremony officiated by a Catholic priest, Brandon and Andrea would recite vows to each other in a ceremony that would be administered by a Protestant pastor.

Each and every invited guest was sent an email informing them to not be shocked; that 'among the guests' would be four jaguars, because they were the de facto house pets of Jungle Cargo and it would be hard to keep them away. It was either let them attend and be a part of it all, or listen to them put up a tremendous, non-stop, distracting roar when penned up. Nobody would want that. It would cover up the sound of the guitars which would replace a conventional organ for wedding intros and music. Every wedding has its own particular problems, and this one certainly has its own!

The reception: Well, that would be held everywhere! The main venue would be the expansive deck. A small wedding orchestra would be set up there with an installed plywood dance floor on top of the decking. The deck was so large that there would still be plenty of room for tables and seating. The one big modification was that food would be served inside the house in the dining room, then taken out to respective guest's tables on the deck. The caterers were very happy with that arrangement, and the guests didn't care, so long as they got to eat.

A bar, however, would be set up on the deck, and so would three separate tables with three beautiful wedding cakes.

Anna Maria and Suyapa also had surprises. On this special day, instead of serving as house maids, the girls were given the day off and asked to be bride's maids. That news brought tears of joy and quite a bit of squealing and happy chatter. Then they were fitted for bride's maid dresses and both of them could not possibly have been prouder.

Basically, the countdown was on. The clock was ticking. The hour grew nigh. On Thursday, June the 18th, Brandon awoke to find a note next to him on Andrea's pillow which read; "Tradition dictates that you cannot see me today before the wedding. I am 'cloistered' in the guest bedroom with my mother, Mary, Leticia, and other women. I love you, my husband to be. See you at 2:00 p.m. Don't be late!"

Brandon read the note, smiled and said to himself, "Now I remember! I knew there was something important I needed to do today!"

At noon, a very muddy, dusty car came speeding into the parking arca, stopped at the base of the stairs, and sat, honking it's horn incessantly. Didier piled out of the passenger door, turned and thanked the driver, then retrieved a suitcase from the back seat. After that, a final thank you was said, with a goodbye wave, and the car backed up, turned and drove away. A tired and dusty looking Didier labored up the stairs, lugging his suitcase.

The honking was heard by Anna Maria who rushed to open the door and spotted the ascending Didier on the stairs. She had seen enough pictures of him on Andrea's camera to know who he was.

She clapped her hands together excitedly and said, "Oui! Bienvenidos, Señor Didier! Please come in, come in!"

Greeting were exchanged, then Didier asked, "How much time before the wedding?"

"Not much," Anna Maria said, who was already wearing her bride's maid dress.

"Do you have a shower I can use?" Didier asked.

"Yes," Anna Maria answered, leading Didier to a guest bedroom. "Everyone is going to be so happy to see you!"

Anna Maria tucked Didier away in a guest bedroom and closed the door but kept his arrival to herself. The only evidence was a silly smile. Suyapa wanted to know what was going on. Anna Maria whispered in her ear. Now both of them were giggling with excitement.

Didier appeared from the bedroom a short while later dressed in a very formal blue suit. He stopped long enough for Suyapa to give him a hug and pin a flower on his lapel, then he found his way through the patio doors and down the stairs to the wedding arena, where he found a seat close to the front.

By 2:00 p.m., all three grooms to be were properly adorned in tuxedos, complete with wide cummerbunds, as they stood adjacent to the triple altar and waited for their brides to be to make the trip down the sandy aisle, one by one from the carport to the beach.

By now, all seats in the guest areas were filled with friends and relatives of all three couples. There was light, happy chatter as they waited for the triple ceremony to begin.

It had been decided that the brides would make the trip one at a time, so as not to steal any other bride's thunder. Mary would be first. Leticia, second and Andrea, third.

Mary had no one to give her away, so she asked Didier if he would do the honors, especially since he was originally going to give Andrea away. He gladly accepted with a huge smile. "What am I supposed to do?" he whispered to Mary.

"Just take my arm and walk with me down the aisle, then shake hands with Don and give him my hand. Then step back to your seat."

"Oh! I can do that!" Didier said.

Leticia's family were all there including her parents, aunts, uncles, cousins. It looked like a tribal meeting. And then, there was Andrea, very pregnant and beautiful. Her adoptive father, Tom Granger led her down the aisle and shook hands with Brandon Shaw as he gave his daughter away.

A traditional Jewish wedding chuppah, or canopy, had been installed at the last minute by the Rabbi to cover the middle section of the three altars, in order to conform with Jewish law.

When the Rabbi had introduced the ceremony, he gave Don permission to speak. Don faced Mary and said loud enough for everyone to hear; "The older I have gotten, the more blessings God has seen to bestow upon me. And you, Mary, are the greatest blessing of all. I vow that I will devote myself to you all the days of my life. I will love you, protect you, adore you. And when I have passed from this world, I will love you then also."

Mary then spoke her lines. "Don, my love, my life had no hope, no joy until I met you. The flowers had no color, no sweet smell. I will love you all the days of my life and devote myself completely to you, so help me God."

Then the Rabbi completed the ceremony in Hebrew, reading from the Talmud. The wine glass was broken, and the Rabbi spoke the words, "May your love bless the two of you until the pieces of this wine glass are rejoined."

Then it was Lorenzo and Leticia's turn to be wed. Theirs was a traditional, by the book, beautiful Catholic ceremony, followed by a lot of whooping and hollering when the priest pronounced them man and wife. Lorenzo also made a point of bending Leticia far back for their wedding kiss.

Through all of this, Cisco had refused to move from Lorenzo's right side, even throughout the ceremony, and nobody was foolish enough to try to move him. Perhaps they were afraid, or perhaps it was now accepted that "In this place, there be jaguars!" Brandon was glad in any case that he had sent the notice out about jaguars being present, and that they were welcome wedding guests.

And, speaking of jaguars, at the beginning of the ceremony between Brandon and Andrea, Naja and her cubs gathered around the loving couple and began to roar loudly for several seconds before the ceremony could begin.

"What are they doing?" Andrea whispered to Brandon as she held her bridal bouquet.

"It's the jaguar way of saying they are happy that we are becoming one. Sort of, 'welcome to the family'."

"Oh," Andrea said. "I like that! It's a little loud, but I like it."

Then the pastor began the official ceremony, that is, as soon as he stopped shaking from all of the roaring, which was happening right at his feet.

"Dearly beloved, we are gathered together, here in the sight of God..."

After the pastor's prep, Brandon turned to Andrea and said, "Throughout our relationship, from time to time you have used the phrase, 'Love is the strongest force on earth.' At first, I did not understand. But you have shown it to be true wisdom so many times, in so many ways. And many times, you have been the one who made it come true because that is who you are. You have taught me how to love, and for that, I will love you for eternity. I proudly take you for my wife, to love, to honor, to share all things with. We are no longer two. From this moment and forever forward, we are one."

Andrea, with her hands in Brandon's hands said, "You reshaped my belief system from the moment I met you. Ironically, I was searching for someone bad. Instead, I found someone good. I thought I was rescuing you. But in truth, it is you who were rescuing me… from myself. I love you, Brandon Shaw. And, so help me God, I will love you forever."

The pastor said, "You have given your troth to one another. Therefore, by the power vested in me, I pronounce that you are husband and wife. Those whom God hath joined together, let no man put asunder."

Brandon and Andrea shared a deep, loving kiss. And then, the party started. As with all celebrations in Latin America, it did not end soon, but rather went deep into the night.

There was one more three-in-one ceremony to perform. All three wedding cakes had to be cut, and wedding pictures taken. Then there were wedding toasts, more pictures, a ceremonial waltz for each couple, more pictures. Andrea made sure that in all the pictures taken, her "something blue" was prominently displayed around her neck, and actually something blue-green; the pendant Didier had given to her long ago, in a faraway place in the Mosquitia Jungle. She also made sure that Didier was in every family group picture.

And speaking of Didier, he was invited to be in all wedding pictures of all three couples. He was family. And it was made clear to him that he held that status. The little man who had no family, did have a family indeed. He was spotted more than once discreetly wiping tears of joy from his eyes. One time, Naja saw him when he was in an emotional state and she went to him to rub her cheek against him. He was loved even by the jaguars.

The orchestra played for hours. People danced until they collapsed in chairs from exhaustion. Then, the orchestra was replaced with a flamenco guitarist and a poet who recited in both English and Spanish. The philosophy of Cervantes was now the music for those who loved poetry, accompanied by Spanish guitar.

Sometime around midnight, the caterers began to wrap things up. By dawn' most signs of the party were history. The company who rented equipment such as the folding chairs and covers showed up to collect their property. Today would be the day everyone would try to get back to normal. Honeymoons would be put in abeyance until after the grand opening of the conservatory.

And that was not the only consideration. Andrea was starting to get close to her delivery date. So, hers and Brandon's honeymoon might have to be put on hold indefinitely.

Besides, when you live a few yards away from the Caribbean, there's no big rush to go on a 'getaway trip'. Where ya gonna go? Closer to the Caribbean? They're already at the Caribbean. How much closer can a person get?

CHAPTER EIGHTEEN

A Premature Birth

In any case, there was little time to think about things like honeymoons. The gift shop was nearing completion and Mary was up to her armpits with ordering merchandise for the store, some of which would be custom made novelties specifically advertising the conservatory.

As if that wasn't enough, Bill Weaver, the bird expert from the San Antonio Zoo had recommended that Jungle Cargo start a large garden to grow their own crop of bird food including sunflower seeds, which, in any case, were hard to come by in Honduras, as well as chili peppers, which were an important part of a parrot's diet. He also recommended okra and other crops of things with large seeds.

Now, a garden had to be plowed and planted. Finding farm workers to prepare the garden wasn't a problem. Getting them to use modern farming techniques was. They were used to slash and burn milpa farming. So, implements to properly clear and prepare the soil needed to be brought in from Tegusigalpa. And then campocinos would need to be trained in how to operate those implements.

About that time, Mary approached Brandon for a meeting while he was sitting at the big square table surrounded by practically everyone in the inner circle.

Mary said, "As much as I love doing things here, and Lord knows I do, there is no way I can handle it all, being the manager of the gift shop and the nutritionist. I'm going to have to choose one, and you're going to have to find somebody to do the other."

Brandon looked at Don. "See! I told you! I was wondering how long it would take her to finally reach that conclusion." Then, to Mary he said, "I completely understand and agree. Which way are you leaning?"

"I love being around those parrots," she confessed. "It's a big responsibility. You need somebody you can depend on. Besides, we've got this bird man from San Antonio down here to train me. We wouldn't want all that training to go to waste. I'll tell you something else, I spent years indoors, caged up in that stupid café. Living day in and day out in half light, smelling grease and yuca root. I want to be outside. I want to breathe the fresh air and smell the flowers. I'll be your nutritionist. Let's find somebody else to be the gift shop manager."

Suddenly, someone at the table spoke up. "I'll do it!" Everybody looked around. It was Leticia. She had her hand in the air. "I like the cedar wood smell inside that building. I like the atmosphere and it isn't even finished yet. I would love to work there. And I think I could do wonders with the place because my head is filled with ideas."

"What about your nursing?" Lorenzo asked.

"You know the truth?" Leticia said. "I'm sick to death of it, right up to here." She indicated by holding the flat of her hand on her forehead. "Besides, if I was working out here, I wouldn't have to bounce back and forth on that nightmare of a road twice a day, going and coming. I hate that pinché road. Ohh! Listen! Now I'm using your words! It would be less wear and tear on our car, *and* me. Tambien, we could have lunch together every day."

"I like that!" Lorenzo said with a smile.

Brandon looked at Andrea, Don, Doug, Francis, Lorenzo and Didier. "Shall we put it to a vote?" he said. "Everybody that's in favor of Leticia running the gift shop, hold up your hand and say Aye."

In unison, everybody held up their hands and said, "Aye!"

"It's a marvelous idea," Andrea said. "Leticia's Spanish is impeccable. Ninety percent of our visitors are going to be Spanish speaking."

"Yeah, but you better get her an assistant that she can train as soon as possible," Mary said with a grin.

"Assistant?" Brandon asked. "Why an assistant?"

"Because, I happen to know that she wants to get knocked up as soon as possible!"

Everyone at the table laughed, except Lorenzo, who looked embarrassed.

"Well, on that note," Didier said, "I had better start figuring out how I'm going to get back to The Jungle Inn. If I go by road, I'm going to need a very thick cushion to put under me. I hate to complain, but that road is something out of a nightmare."

"Tell me about it," Andrea said furtively. "But I have a better idea. Why don't you stay a few more days as our guest, 'for a change', Didier."

"That's the best idea I've heard in a long time," Brandon said. "You know, Andrea is supposed to bingo. Damn! I mean, give birth in the near future. Why not stay here long enough for that?"

Didier smiled broadly. "I… I would be greatly honored. Oh, thank you. I accept your invitation. I just need to use your computer to send my crew a message that I will be delayed."

"Sure," Andrea said. "I'll show you where the computer is and make sure the internet is working."

It was at that very moment that Naja's cubs suddenly started stirring as if something was bothering them. As in so many times previously, they flanked Andrea and assumed a position as if on guard. This did not go unnoticed by anyone at the table, and Brandon began to get slightly nervous, looking out at the yard and beach for any sign of trouble. Nothing could be seen, but something was definitely upsetting the jaguar cubs.

Brandon then used his special communicative ability to try and probe the cub's minds, but whatever they were thinking was unclear. Was there danger? No, it didn't feel like danger. Something else? Most likely. But what?

Leticia wanted to brush off the behavior of the cubs. She was excited about her new official position and was anxious now to go to the gift shop to visit, albeit now from a new perspective. Everyone decided a visit to the unfinished gift shop would be fun, so they started to get up from their chairs at the table. Andrea and Didier would join them as soon as Didier completed his email. That's when it happened.

Andrea was half-way out of her chair when suddenly she was hit with a sharp pain in her abdomen area. She let out a scream and sank back down into the chair, grabbing at her stomach.

Leticia looked alarmed. "Oh God, I think she's going into labor!"

Andrea's friend and nurse rushed to her side. "Let's get her inside quickly, out of this heat," Leticia said.

With Brandon on one side of her and Leticia on the other, they managed to get Andrea out of the lawn chair and into the house quickly. They took her straight to the bedroom to lie down.

"Do you still have the pain," Leticia asked.

Andrea shook her head, no.

"There is no way she is going to travel down that bullshit La Ceiba road in a fucking car or Jeep, or worse, a truck," Leticia said. Then she immediately got on her cell phone and called the doctor. After quickly explaining what was happening with Andrea, and why Leticia was afraid to move her, she hung up the phone. "Doctor Jimenez is on her way," she said.

Actually, Doctor Sofia Jimenez had been a wedding guest and was at the house less than forty-eight hours previously. So, she knew exactly where she was headed. This might help with response time.

Just at that moment, Tom Granger walked in, having been awakened from his afternoon nap. "What's going on?" he asked.

"Andrea might be going into labor," Mary answered.

Tom Granger's response was to turn and run through the house yelling, "Sarah! Sarah? Come quick? Where are you?"

Andrea clutched at her midriff harder as another spasm of pain hit her. Leticia was at her side, trying to help. But there was little she could do. And the jaguar cubs were in the way. They were flanking the bed on either side and doing a good job of making nuisances of themselves. Brandon finally had to intervene and take the cubs outside, much to their objection.

Leticia left Andrea's side for a moment and half whispered to Brandon, "I hope the doctor gets here soon. I don't think this is a normal labor."

"What do you mean?" Brandon demanded.

"I mean that her labor pains are not normal. Something else is going on."

"Brandon?" Andrea yelled.

He rushed to her side and held her hand. "I'm here, Baby."

"Don't let them take me to a hospital, please. I hate hospitals. Let me have this baby here at home."

"Only if it's an absolute emergency," Brandon said.

"There couldn't be any emergency that dire," Andrea said, obviously in pain.

Leticia got on the phone again. "Doctor Sofia? Yes, Leticia. How far away are you?"

"I'm at least fifteen minutes away," the doctor said. "And now, there's a rain-storm coming down off the mountain-side. I hope I reach you before the rain starts."

The doctor had been on Leticia's speaker-phone, so Lorenzo, Didier and others had heard. "Aye, chihuahua! A pinché rain-storm?" Lorenzo rushed to the back door and swung it open so he could peer toward the mountains.

"Yep, here it comes. That cloud is almost black. It's gonna be a good one. I just hope we don't lose electricity."

"Don't even say that out loud," Brandon said, almost too softly.

Andrea let out another scream. Leticia rushed to her side. "Doctor Sofia is almost here," Leticia said, trying to comfort Andrea.

"Don't let her take me to the hospital," Andrea repeated. "I want to have this baby here, in this house."

"Listen, we will not move you unless your life depends on it. But if it comes to that, we aren't going to have any choice. You need to understand."

"If you try to take me out of this house, those jaguars will attack."

"What do you mean? How do you know that?"

"I don't know how I know. I just know."

"Oh shit," Leticia said as she looked up at Brandon.

"Don't ask me," he said. "But they do seem pretty stirred up. I mean… is she going to be safe, having the baby here?"

"That isn't for me to say," Leticia answered.

A few minutes later, the doctor's car pulled up in back of the house and she came rushing up the stairs with her medical bag in hand. Leticia was waiting for her with an open door. A very loud clap of thunder announced the rain-storm's arrival.

"Thank God you're here," Tom Granger said. "Listen, I want the best care my daughter can have. Money is no object…"

Lorenzo, who happened to be the one standing closest to Tom Granger when he started chattering, turned on him and said, "Oh, why don't you sit down and shut the fuck up, old man? Do you think this woman would give Andrea anything other than the best possible care? You're stupid, you know that? Pendejo!" Lorenzo issued the command with such vehemence that Tom immediately closed his mouth. No one else in the house said a word in contradiction.

Dr. Sofia went directly into the bedroom where she found Andrea in extreme pain. She asked Leticia's help in getting Andrea's vitals and some other exams.

Meanwhile, she turned to everyone else in the bedroom and said, "It would help a lot if all of you would go into the other room. I'll call any of you if I need you."

With that, everyone shuffled out of the bedroom, leaving the doctor and the nurse to do their work.

Andrea could be heard uttering cries of pain from time to time. Presumably when labor pains hit her. By now thunder was right on top of the house making so much noise that it sounded like the Apocalypse and rattled the dishes. Rain pattered hard on the roof.

"Well, now we find out whether the roofers did their job right or not," Don said, trying to lighten the mood a little.

The bedroom door opened, and Dr. Sofia came out, looking concerned. She approached Brandon, stood there a moment, then said, "It's a breech baby."

"What's that?" Brandon asked.

"Uh, the baby is in the wrong position inside the womb. That kind of birth can be problematic."

"Problematic is not the word I want to be hearing right now."

"Never-the-less, that's the situation and we don't have any choice except to deal with it. That baby is coming into the world, whether we are ready or not. Now, whether it arrives safely depends on what we do."

"Which is?"

"The safest thing, Brandon, is to take the baby via caesarean birth. Do you have any problem with that?"

"You mean, where you cut her belly open?"

"That's what I mean. Otherwise she is going to lie there and suffer. Breech isn't her only problem. I mean, we might be able to work with that, maybe not. But she also isn't dilating the way she is supposed to."

"Why not?"

"Because she's a woman in her late thirties and she has never had a child before. It's a common problem in mothers her age."

"Damn. You make her sound old."

"Excuse me, but we don't have time for chit chat. What I'm recommending is caesarean section and I need your permission. You are her husband, and you have to make the call."

At that moment, Tom Granger piped up. "I am her father, and I will make the call!"

Whereupon, Lorenzo stepped forward and without warning, hit Tom Granger as hard as he could, smack in the face, breaking his nose and sending him flying backwards across the dining-room floor. "Shut up," Lorenzo said. "You ain't calling nothing, except maybe a taxi."

Mary stepped forward and took Lorenzo's hand. "That was awfully hard, Lorenzo. Is your hand alright?" Lorenzo nodded yes, and then winked at Mary.

"Are you going to have to take her to the hospital?" Brandon asked. "I mean, she's made it very clear that she doesn't want to go, if there's any way of avoiding it."

"I know," Dr. Sofia said. "She's talked about that many times during our visits. That's why I brought some extra instruments and supplies. It's a little late to try to move her now, anyway."

Thunder rolled and lightning struck not too far from the house.

"What can I do to help?" Brandon asked.

"You can go to my car and grab another big black bag that's in the back seat. After that, you might want to keep flashlights handy just in case we lose power while I'm in the middle of this procedure."

"I'll go get the bag," Lorenzo said. He was out the door in a blur.

Five minutes later, Dr. Sofia was explaining to Andrea what was about to happen.

"Just don't take me to a hospital," Andrea pleaded.

"The only way I will do that is if you start to hemorrhage," the doctor said. "The only thing I have here is a local anesthetic. I am going to administer this. Sorry, but you're going to feel the needle. Then, we're going to make a portal and take that baby out of you, safe and sound."

Although she was frightened, she wasn't about to show it. She felt the pain as Dr. Sofia injected the needle with the anesthetic, but after that, she felt nothing in her stomach area. She saw the doctor with her surgical mask and gloves, she saw the scalpel, but never felt the cut, although she knew that is what was happening.

Then, in what was a magic moment, she saw the baby being lifted out of her. She was so dizzy that she couldn't get a good look at it. Dr. Sofia and Leticia looked at one another as they cut the umbilical cord, washed the baby and then showed it to Andrea before wrapping it in a swaddling blanket. The next several minutes were spent carefully closing the opening made in Andrea's stomach area, and uterus. Dr. Sofia made the stitches as small as possible.

Andrea thought she remembered being conscious during this part of the procedure, but she kept fading in and out. She was relieved because the baby was safe. The dangerous part was over.

Now, although extremely dizzy, Andrea smiled, looking into the face of her child. Then she noticed something.

"What's wrong with his little hands?" she asked in a slurred voice.

"Why nothing at all," Dr. Sofia said. "They're little jaguar claws, just like his ancient ancestors. Aren't they pretty?"

Andrea began to scream bloody murder. She continued to scream. She didn't know how long she screamed, until Dr. Sofia woke her up, saying, "Andrea, Andrea, what's the matter?"

"Where's my baby?" she pleaded.

"Right here, Honey," Brandon said. He was standing

only a couple of feet away, cradling the baby with a proud smile on his face. "If it's alright with you, I want to name him, Brandon Junior."

"I want to see his hands," Andrea said in desperation.

"Sure," Brandon said. "They are so tiny!" Brandon unwrapped the blanket so a tiny arm could be freed to show Andrea the hand. "Five little fingers, so small they can hardly hold on to my finger," the proud father said with a smile.

Andrea desperately looked at Little Brandon's hand and saw that it was perfectly normal. There was no claw. She had been dreaming. Her expression suddenly softened. "Can I hold my baby?" she asked.

"Of course," Dr. Sofia said. Brandon handed Andrea the baby, ever so tenderly.

"I am a father," Brandon said with pride. Andrea cradled her newborn child and looked at it with love.

"You can name him Brandon Junior," Andrea said. "But I want his middle name to be Didier."

"Didier it is!" Brandon announced.

At that moment, as if on que, Didier appeared in the bedroom door, hands over his mouth, tears in his eyes. "Does that make me '*Uncle*' Didier?" he asked.

"It certainly does," Andrea said. "Come meet your nephew."

CHAPTER NINETEEN

Transition Complete!

EIGHT MONTHS LATER, BRANDON, ANDREA, BABY BRANDON and three jaguars sat in a new, covered, six passenger golf cart, near the newly opened gift shop of the new Jungle Cargo Conservatory, waving at visitors boarding a twenty passenger electric tour cart driven by a very professional looking guide, who was dressed in a khaki safari shirt, logo patches on the sleeves, and shorts, and wearing a safari hat, with a knife on his belt.

"Okay everyone, get comfortable and be sure to buckle your seat belts," the guide said, as he walked the length of the vehicle, checking to make sure everyone was in incompliance.

"This tour through the jungle takes about forty-five minutes. You're going to learn things about parrots and macaws that you never imagined, including, why this jungle cannot survive without them. We will have one rest stop along the way. Aside from that, please do not leave the vehicle. Okay, here we go. Enjoy!"

With that, the electric tour kart started to move

forward, and the guide inserted the English language CD. Andrea had helped write the script, and because she had a velveteen voice, she had been asked to record both the English and Spanish versions of the pre-recorded tour.

"Many secrets are hidden within the darkness of the jungle," the CD began.

Baby Brandon, strapped into his car seat in the golf cart, and wearing blue rimmed sunglasses, smiled and kicked, as all happy babies do. Andrea got a far-away look in her eyes.

"What's the matter," Bandon asked.

"Not a thing in the world," Andrea answered with a smile. "I was just thinking back to the first day I met you, in the La Ceiba airport, looking like barbequed dog mess. I don't think anyone who saw you that day would recognize you today."

"Well," Brandon mused. "That's probably a good thing. Don't you think?"

"Yeah, but do you ever miss being Lord of the Jungle, king of your realm?"

"Who says I'm not still Lord of the Jungle? And now I have Jane and Boy."

Brandon turned halfway around, so he could address the jaguars. "What do you guys say? Am I still Lord of the Jungle?"

When Brandon said that, all three jaguars began to roar at the top of their very loud, thunderous voices. You would think a racket like that would have frightened Baby Brandon, but he just smiled broadly, and laughed as he looked up at his father.

THE END

THANK YOU FOR READING

Did you enjoy this book?

We invite you to leave a review at your favorite book site, such as Goodreads, Amazon, Barnes & Noble, etc.

DID YOU KNOW THAT LEAVING A REVIEW…

- Helps other readers find books they may enjoy.
- Gives you a chance to let your voice be heard.
- Gives authors recognition for their hard work.
- Doesn't have to be long. A sentence or two about why you liked the book will do.

ABOUT THE AUTHOR

GEORGE DISMUKES spent the first half of his life in pursuit of adventure. This ranged from bullfighting as a youth to milking poisonous snakes professionally at Ross Allen's Reptile Institute in Silver Springs, Florida. The early 60s found him pursuing wild animals across the Serengeti in the movie business and operating an animal export company in Iquitos, Peru.

He spent many years exploring archaeological sites of the ancient Maya Indians in Central America and studying their lost civilization. He also lived in Honduras, where the story, TWO FACES OF THE JAGUAR, and THE LOST CITY take place.

In 1980, he began a video production company in Houston, Texas and worked as a 'triple threat' (writer/director/producer) creating some of the Houston market's most creative television commercials. He won a CLEO award for his production of a series of television

PSAs concerning prevention of child abuse, funded through a grant from the University of Houston.

Currently, he lives on the Texas Coast with his soul mate and closest friend, Nadine, where he writes and works in magazine advertising. His hobbies include growing exotic chili peppers and experimenting with salsa recipes. Above all, George is a devout animal lover and advocate, fighting against animal abuse. He has two dogs, named Pulga and Gizmo, respectively.

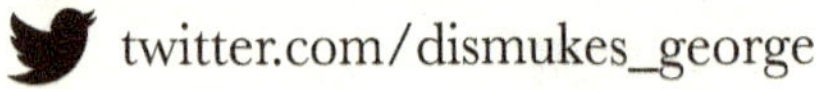

ALSO BY GEORGE DISMUKES

Two Faces of the Jaguar

The Lost City

Jaguar's Quest

Siren Song (coming soon)

www.ingramcontent.com/pod-product-compliance
Lightning Source LLC
LaVergne TN
LVHW090944080826
845145LV00003B/881

* 9 7 8 1 9 5 3 7 3 5 6 3 8 *